Paradise Affirmed

Paradise Affirmed

Stories of Virtue and Scandal at Happy
Corner Church

Nancy Werking Poling

Screech Owl Press

"Afterlife" appeared in Persimmon Tree No.52, Spring 2020.

"Paradise Affirmed" was previously published as "Intrusion" in Wholeness: A Wising Up Anthology, Wising up Press, 2023.

"Paradise Misconstrued" was previously published as "A Sunday Intrusion" in Wild Crone Wisdom, Wild Librarian Press, 2023.

Published by:
Screech Owl Press,
624 Azalea Ave.,
Black Mountain, NC 28711

www.oldmp.com
Old Mountain Press eBook Division
www.oldmp.com/e-book

CONTENTS

Eden's Decline

THE HAPPY CORNER Baptist Church was located in what had once been a prosperous neighborhood with sturdy brick houses and tree-shaded sidewalks. Prominent civic leaders of the past rested in the adjoining cemetery, among them former mayor Estes Harlan (1821-1883). Passersby marked the seasons by the hedge bordering church and cemetery. Fisted yellow-green clusters in early spring, red bursts of leaves in the fall, skeletal gray branches through the winter.

The building, according to the historical marker on Oak Street, was constructed in 1881 on land donated by William P. Farley, founder of the Farley Buggy Company. Its exterior, massive gray blocks of masonry with two symmetrically placed towers, gave the sense of an imposing fortress designed to keep enemies from storming the faithful.

Inside, pew cushions covered in faded red velvet offered minimal comfort; a frayed red carpet ran up the center aisle. Two of the stained-glass windows were authentic Tiffanies, scenes from the twenty-third Psalm extolling green pastures and gently flowing streams. However, the windows weren't the focus of attention when one entered the cavernous sanctuary. No, like the golden idol of King Nebuchadnezzar, the organ's enormous polished pipes behind the altar commanded, if not worship, at least awe.

For more than a century the Happy Corner Baptist Church had been an all-white congregation. Many members lived near enough to walk to Sunday morning services; others drove a short distance. In the 1970s a few professional Black families bought homes in the community, which allowed realtors to plant fears that property values would soon plummet. They

1

urged homeowners to sell before it was too late. A self-fulfilling prophecy.

The few remaining members reached out to the newcomers. They distributed welcoming flyers door-to-door and sponsored hospitable events, such as ice cream socials. Neighboring Black Christians either already had a church or didn't find a good spiritual fit at the Happy Corner Baptist Church.

Those faithful who remained: The Melrose family, Stella and Tom Hamilton, Miriam Slaughbaugh, Horace Jenkins, Holly and Roland Martin, Felicia Farmer, Phyllis Baxter, Wade and Elsie Kirkakoff, to name a few of the forty-five members. Salt of the earth, these people were.

A poll, had one been taken, would have found that most of them, Phyllis Baxter definitely the exception, agreed that God was male, that a baptizee had to be dunked backward one time. They believed they would be reunited with loved ones in heaven, bodies intact.

ALTHENA MELROSE SANG in a blaring alto, her gaze turned heavenward, "My Jesus, I lo-uve Thee, I know Thou art mine." Standing beside her, not taking his eyes off the black ellipses on the hymnal page, her twelve-year-old son Jason nervously carried the melody. Wavering tenor tones came from Tom, the older Melrose boy, whose voice was changing. Hank, the family patriarch, projected his booming bass out over the heads of the congregation.

"My Je-e-sus 'tis now" faded, and as the Melrose family filed into the seventh row of pews, Tom deliberately stumbled into his younger brother, who in turn accidently bumped into their mother. Althena lurched forward and hit her funny bone on the back of the pew in front of her. "Oh crap!" she said louder than intended. Tom's face turned so red in embarrassment that his acne blotches stood out all the more.

A few members remembered the days when the church had a paid organist and a choir whose anthems inspired sacred sighs. Now the Melrose family provided most of the special music.

Once in a while Horace Jenkins's daughter, who'd taken voice lessons twenty years earlier, came to town. She was usually willing to sing one or two selections, always classical. Her vibrato set the handful of children to giggling, and parents to shushing their offspring, a disruption to the worshipful attitude the music was intended to evoke. Horace, though, would close his eyes and sway his head back and forth in reverie.

At Pastor Bill's summons—hands uplifted—the congregation stood, hymnals open. Stella Hamilton's fingers stumbled across the organ keys. (She avoided the pedals.) The hymn had two sharps, so she made a lot of mistakes. Partway through, when she got so confused that she had to stop playing altogether, everybody kept right on singing. They knew that after a few measures she'd be able to pick up the accompaniment again. Sensitive to Stella's musical limitations, Pastor Bill usually selected songs without sharps, but "Guide me, O Thou Great Jehovah" went remarkably well with his sermon title, "Treading the Verge of Jordan."

On the floor, at Miriam Slaughbaugh's feet, lay her seeing-eye dog, Freckles, a golden retriever. His eyelids drooping, drooping, drooping still further until only a narrow sliver of eye was visible. Now and then he jerked, opened his eyes wide, shook his head so vigorously that his tags jingled. Each time Miriam made a loud *shhh* and patted him on the head.

Pastor Bill didn't sound all that inspired this morning. In his defense it had been a busy week, what with two funerals leaving little time to work on a sermon. So he was pretty much thinking on his feet, adding a few ideas that hadn't come to him the night before. It seemed that when he had the least to say he dragged things out the longest. More than likely Marsha would tell him this afternoon, "It just wasn't up to your usual quality."

Given the stifling air and Pastor Bill's lack of inspiration, hardly anyone followed what he intended to be a three-point sermon but was dragging out to five. Those who were awake mostly contemplated their problems. Marylou Abbott worried about Langford's eternal soul, given he refused to attend church with her. Oda MacFarland worried about the throng of communists in the country. Phyllis Baxter worried about the Orioles' losing streak.

As soon as Stella played the first note of the closing hymn, Freckles, like the humans around him, stirred. His tags rattled as he moved into the center aisle, where he lay down to nap some more while the congregation ended the service with "Come, Thou Fount of Every Blessing." A hymn that was supposed to be sung with vigor, but with Stella at the organ, every song advanced at about the same slow tempo.

Relieved that one more Sunday sermon was finished, Bill stepped down from the pulpit and recited, "The Lord bless you and keep you. The Lord make . . ." Freckles stood at attention and waited for the benediction's amen, the signal that it was time to lead Miriam out the side door. A routine left over from the days when the sanctuary had been packed on Sunday mornings and Miriam worried about getting disoriented by all the commotion.

Everyone else exited by way of the vestibule, through the nine-foot-high front doors made of solid oak. So accustomed were church members passing through that they seldom bothered to examine the Eden drama unfolding in intricate carvings along the doors' borders. A man, a woman, a tempter, a tropical tree heavy laden with fruit that offered discernment. The whole story was there, the drama of disobedience and lies, of humankind going down the drain.

The Fall

Regions of sorrow, doleful shades, where peace
And rest can never dwell, hope never comes
That comes to all; but torture without end.
Paradise Lost, Book I, lines 65-67.

GOD, FORGIVE ME; God, forgive me; God, forgive me. In the third pew from the back of the sanctuary, on a frayed red velvet pad, he sits with bowed head, hands clasped. Not in prayer, for he long ago quit believing in the power of prayer. Leaving one to wonder why he gets up, showers and shaves, puts on his navy-blue blazer and paisley tie and walks six blocks to church. Every Sunday.

Pastor Bill and Marsha have been kind to him, inviting him over to the parsonage for dinner, letting him be silent or curse, depending on his mood. Marsha finds clothes for him at Goodwill, and Pastor Bill arranged for a therapist. Bill and Marsha have become family.

On a May Sunday, along the way to church, he doesn't notice the forsythia, its bright yellow blossoms shouting for attention. Doesn't see the hedge bordering the cemetery with its chartreuse leaves. Doesn't feel the warmth of the morning sun or smell the newness of the grass.

Another day in May. The fear, the fear of death—his own and that of others. Sweat under his protective gear.

Remorse. He's willed it away, tried to pray it away, but it hovers over him like the clouds of tear gas. Not dissipating, though, not dissipating at all.

God, forgive me; God, forgive me; God, forgive me.

From the mighty organ dominating the front of the sanctuary—its discordant full-throttle reverberations rumbling through his body—comes what's supposed to be a melody of triumph. He's advancing up the hill, bayonet pointed. Onward Christian soldiers, marching as to war. *As* to war.

Killing should come as natural to an Ohio farm boy as butchering a hog. Thrusting a knife to the heart, scalding the carcass. But come butchering time he'd hidden in a closet, teeth chattering while he sat on the floor hugging his knees. Wouldn't help kill chickens either, them flapping their wings so frantically and squawking. They felt fear, he knew they did. Then you should be a vegetarian, his sister told him.

He stares ahead at the organ, its pipes not reaching toward the high ceiling as usual but aiming like gun barrels at the congregation. He's standing up there clinging to one, pointing it, pulling the trigger. He takes a deep breath, counts slowly to ten as Glenda has told him to do. He turns to the Tiffany window nearby, searching for solace in the green pasture, the still waters, trying, as Pastor Bill instructs the congregation, to affirm life. Why? Because it is a gift from God and isn't spring beautiful and just think of all the opportunities we have to be of service to God and neighbor and halleluiah praise the Lord.

How can he affirm his own life when he has taken it from another?

HE LETS LOOSE a string of goddamns, lowers the TV control with a forceful flip of the wrist, and plunges the screen into blackness. Anniversaries are to be celebrated. Bring out the champagne, pop the corks, clink the glasses. Say *l'chaim*, or *prost* or *santé* or whatever they utter on some distant shore where they have no reason to remember, no pictures that draw them back to a past that even at the time made no sense.

He doesn't need TV commentators to remind him. For thirty years not a day passes that he doesn't see the images. Not a day that he hasn't moaned God, forgive me; God, forgive me;

6

God, forgive me. There's no escape from the screams, the shouts, the blood.

He was just a kid. There because he didn't want to die in a rice paddy on the other side of the Earth. Didn't want to kill either. God, forgive me; God, forgive me; God, forgive me.

—I have come that you might have life and have it more abundantly.

If we obey the commandments and try to be like Jesus, Pastor Bill claims, our lives will be filled with peace and joy. Words coming from a man no more than thirty who's seen nothing of the real world.

Well, it ain't like that, Pastor, not like that at all. Just start going down the list of thou-shalt-nots and pretty soon you get it. Oh, the first ones are easy. Honor God, don't make any graven images. Taking the Lord's name in vain, that's a minor infraction. Every man does it. Anyway, no big ear's suspended up in the sky listening to each word that comes out of my mouth.

As far back as he can remember he's kept the Sabbath holy. In one of all those albums Mama compiled of his growing up years, there's a certificate for regular attendance in Cradle Roll. And he was the first to get baptized in the inside baptistery of the church back home. Came up teeth chattering because whoever installed it didn't think to include a warmwater valve.

Thou shalt not kill. Thou shalt not kill.

After the service Wilbur McDougal comes up to him, looking every bit his seven-plus decades, with an unreliable memory that's forgotten they've talked before. Posture bent over, bushy white eyebrows to match the hair on his head, he speaks in raspy voice.

—You're the kid who got out of going to Nam, ain't you?

Wilbur tugs at his shirt tail, lifts it to reveal a five-inch scar. Right there in the sanctuary.

—See this? A badge of honor. I fought for my country. Yes sir-ee, some of us weren't cowards.

Obey the commandments. Experience the abundant life that Jesus offers.

Glenda sits in her swivel chair, pen in hand poised over a yellow legal pad, waiting for him to spill his guts. Her saying he can't get over all these feelings of guilt unless he talks about them. Patty saying the same thing—it had to have been twenty years ago—her saying whatever's been eating at you all these years keeps you from forming close relationships and if you don't deal with the crap, this marriage is going to end up like your other two. Turned out to be an accurate prediction.

So he talks about it, blathering on and on, sometimes speechless while he sobs into his hands, while Glenda hands him a box of tissues and sits there nodding yes like she understands when he knows she doesn't.

He tried telling Maribelle once.

—I was just a kid.

He stopped. Like a nineteen-year-old isn't responsible for his actions? There was no command. They were on edge, afraid even though they had M-1s with bayonets and the students only had rocks and teargas canisters. His neighbor's son Max, he's in college, smart as blazes. An Eagle Scout who knows the difference between right and wrong and knows to wait before you act and how to keep a cool head.

—In Jesus Christ you are forgiven.

Every Sunday Pastor Bill, with God-bestowed authority granted because he went to seminary and has all the papers to signify holy clout, raises his hand and pronounces the forgiveness of sins.

Words, just words.

He has long wished for a scar like the one Wilbur McDougal has, a big one that runs across his face for everyone to see. Yet here he is in sound health without so much as high blood pressure. Maybe that's God's revenge. Maybe God will force him to live a long life of mental torment. He has sinned. He deserves to die.

—Crucify him! Crucify him!

Though they have no need to fear this man who preaches love of neighbor and peace.

They weren't a violent group. Yes, a few were throwing rocks and beer cans. Yes, some were drinking and rowdy. But the troops felt threatened, even though they were the ones with bayonets, rifles, and protective armor.

Hell, no, we won't go. Don't trust anyone over thirty. Don't trust the Establishment.

He and his disciples, they were anti-establishment too, standing up to the authorities.

—Put down your sword. We won't resort to violence.

What do you think you're doing, you Roman guys, killing the savior of the world?

This land is our land, from California to the . . . We claim our voice. We will speak out against the government. We plant our bodies on this spot. We shall not be moved. We shall not be moved.

He had a gun. He was only a kid, no older than those he faced. They taunted him. They called him a mother-fucker. A sell-out. They threw bottles. They set fires. The governor said they were commies.

He had a gun.

All the guys were avoiding the war the best way they could. George crossed the border into Canada. Stayed there. Hal knocked up Annie so he could say he had a child and shouldn't have to go. Larry went to seminary because ministerial students got deferred, as did rich kids who knew a senator. Some even paid a doctor to say they had a condition that made them unfit for combat.

The government didn't want to leave the homeland unprotected. For one weekend a month, two weeks in the summer, he was trained to kill. In case the U.S. was invaded. Still, Daddy called him a coward.

Sometimes he thinks of all the secrets that will die with him. Most of them of no interest to others. A memory of holding Anna Marie Appleton close at a high school dance and getting a hard-on. The nude pictures he hid under his mattress. He knows he can be forgiven for boyish lust. But what he did on that May day. Four were killed.

He's visited several churches, hoping someone will offer absolution he can accept. Convince me, Preacher, that I am forgiven. He kneels, he weeps, he takes communion. He can find no one, though, whom he trusts to speak for God. Not even Pastor Bill.

—You've got something I just can't reach.

Barbara thought all you have to do is talk about it and once he told a therapist his secrets everything would be right between him and Barbara. Go to a shrink and tell where that God-awful pain is coming from. That's all you've got to do.

The smell of Glenda's office has become familiar. The treated leather of the recliner he leans back in. The peppermint candy she sucks on to camouflage her smoker's breath.

Camouflage. It convinced him he was a man of courage who would defend his country. Polished black boots. A gas mask. A combat helmet. For chrissake, he didn't even know where Vietnam was.

Protect the homeland while the real heroes are on the other side of the globe. Defend it from eighteen, nineteen, twenty-year-old American kids.

He kneels and lowers his rifle. He doesn't think. He aims, he fires. In front of him there's running and screaming. Over by the sidewalk a body lies on the ground. Motionless.

If I had a hammer, I'd hammer out justice, I'd hammer out free-ee-dom.

But he had a gun. He had a gun because he didn't want to die in a rice paddy on the other side of the Earth.

I'd hammer out love between . . .

Paradise Misconceived

AN ALARM SOUNDS. Everyone on the cruise ship is racing toward a lifeboat. Sea waves wash over the deck, lightning flashes across the night sky. I try to scream but it's as if my mouth is stuffed with rags. My muffled moan startles me awake. It's not an alarm to abandon ship but the buzz of my front doorbell. I've fallen asleep in front of the TV. Foggy-eyed, I check the score before rising from my recliner. Bears—13, Raiders—0. The same as it was when I fell asleep.

At the front door I put my eye to the peephole and regard teenagers in parkas. For twenty-seven years I faced adolescents daily, won the hearts of some, the disdain of a few. I open the door without hesitation. Before me stand six kids, all of them white, three girls and three boys. Each one well-scrubbed, like they're auditioning for a McDonald's commercial. I gaze up and down the street through the top of my bifocals. No cars are parked within sight. Did these kids just drop out of the heavens? I stand in the doorway, neither in nor out, which doesn't commit me to engage in conversation.

"Hello, ma'am," a tall girl with a ponytail says. "We're from Bethel Community Church up in Philadelphia, and our youth group is collecting cans of food for the poor." The boy beside her lifts a plastic bag. "Would you like to contribute?"

Now, why are six teenagers from Philadelphia collecting food more than a hundred miles from home when suburbs wealthier than this surround their own city? From my TV come cheers, like somebody's made a touchdown.

I yawn then grumble what I hope will send these kids on their way: "Sorry, I already donate to our local food bank."

A boy in a stocking cap steps forward, a trace of fuzz on his chin. Probably about sixteen. He flashes a wide smile, revealing

11

the shimmering metal of braces. His tone is respectful as he glances down at a clipboard. "We'd like to ask you a few questions, if you don't mind."

I'm loath to discourage altruistic kids. "Shoot, but make it snappy."

"Do you go to church?"

What the—? No wonder I don't see a car; they probably came here in a bus. This isn't altruism; it's evangelizing. I remember the lingo: witness, salvation, sin. They probably want to convert the whole neighborhood.

"Yes." There's more cheering in the background. I want to see what's going on.

"Which one?"

I point toward downtown. "Happy Corner. Thanks for—" I don't get the chance to add *stopping by.*

A girl has already stepped forward. She's short, on the plump side, with a sweet smile that reminds me of—what was her name? Jenny something. This girl asks, "What two words would you use to describe your relationship with God?"

I repeat, "Two words?" Anyone who knows me will tell you I'm not one for brevity.

The six stand there staring at me expectantly. It's cold in this realm between inside and outside, youth and not-so-young. I want to get rid of them. "Lifelong—though it's one word. My daddy was a minister." I've not described my relationship with God, which would involve more of what I don't believe than what I do.

As if the group has rehearsed this conversation, the boy in the stocking cap asks, "What is your concept of God?"

I remember being their age, positive I had this God business figured out. Right now I could speak my truth: that the older you get the less certain you are about the Almighty. That simple answers don't cut it anymore. But if I say anything about God as an ambiguous presence—first of all, "ambiguous presence" will mean nothing to them—who doesn't necessarily know everything and isn't powerful enough to have kept the Nazis from killing Jews or Americans from spreading napalm across Vietnam. If I mention such ideas, I'll be spending the rest of the afternoon arguing with these kids.

"Well now, I'd rather not answer that."

A girl reaches in and gently tugs on the sleeve of my sweatshirt. Our eyes meet. Hers speak out for . . . for . . . No, they don't speak. They scream. Over the years I saw similar signs of unhappiness and suffering in the eyes of students. Is it all in my head, or is she asking for more than perfunctory answers to questions on a clipboard? Her world is out of sync. Something in what she's being taught doesn't resonate. She wants an adult to speak forthrightly.

I grew up in the fifties, not all that great an era if you were female. If you had doubts and your minister-father thought he had all the answers. It's a strange time to think of my high school friend, Linda. Of the night when she tugged at my sleeve. We were seniors and sat cross-legged in the middle of her double bed, hair in curlers, discussing the Meaning of Life. She stood and walked over to the window. Her hands grasping the two venetian-blind cords, she opened then closed the slats, opened then closed them again. She turned to face me.

Her voice quivered. "Do you know what a lesbian is?"

I hesitated, uncomfortable about where the conversation might lead. "Yeah."

She cleared her throat. "I am one." Paused before adding, "I have a girlfriend." She stepped toward me. Her voice choked, she asked, "Do you think I'll go to hell?"

At that moment, like a fault in Earth's crust, a deep chasm opened in my heart. A giant divide between God the judge who sent people to hell and God who loved everyone and protected them. It was the latter one I acknowledged. "No, I don't think you'll go to hell." But the people at church turned against Linda, told her she should repent. She quit coming to church and Daddy wouldn't let me spend time with her anymore. All of these memories flash before me right after the girl at my door has held onto my sleeve and peered into my eyes.

"We'd like to keep you in our prayers," a boy says. "Do you have any concerns we can pray about?"

I struggle to divert my attention from the girl. My chuckle is condescending, bitter even. I've got plenty of concerns. Pray for my retirement fund, I want to say, that it won't run out. Pray my old Jetta doesn't croak. Pray that the Middle East doesn't blow up, that the planet won't be destroyed by global warming.

Pray for Linda, that she found a partner worthy of her and that they live in a friendly place where her gifts are affirmed.

"No, not really." I step back inside the doorway to signal that I'm finished. The strangers thank me politely and turn to leave. The girl with the aching dark eyes briefly lingers.

I sense her disappointment. Or maybe I've imagined that she wants me to speak with honesty. In any case, I close the door and return to the football game.

Pandemonium

SHIT! SHIT! SHIT! Can't say it out loud, though. Denied the luxury of profanity by profession and a mother who'd have washed my mouth out with soap.

A plaster ankle-to-midthigh cast on my leg. Leg propped on a chair. Body twisted like the licorice Twizzlers Marsha gave out at Halloween. Quit feeling sorry for yourself, Bill, and get started. Why'd I agree to write this? Because old geezers like Oda are just about the only ones left in this church.

Ministering to the Elderly. What if I tell the truth? Write about sitting in this very chair when in comes Wade Kirkakoff? Ever since he got elected chair of the Buildings and Grounds Committee, he's been after me to do one thing or another. As if resurrection's in my job description. Cancer of the Edifice. Disintegrating, limb by limb. Leak by leak. Crumble by crumble. Rot by rot.

"I want you to see this." I could tell by the scrunch of his bristly brown eyebrows that he was in pain.

"Can't it wait? I'm in prayer." Always a showstopper. Nobody wants to come between a pastor and his God.

"No, I've just made a very disturbing discovery."

I expected a leak in the roof or a busted water pipe. Instead, Wade leads me into the long, narrow room off the chancel. First day on the job I opened the door, looked around, closed the door, and never went back in. Mildew odor like nobody bothered to take the bedrolls off the Ark. A combination of Grandma's attic and the junkyard out on Route 16. Pews pushed against the wall, piled high with plastic flowers and tarnished urns. Stacks of old hymnals and papers.

Wade pointed down at the floor. "Look." A mound of floral-patterned draperies had been pulled aside to reveal a large, discolored aluminum cylinder.

"What?"

Wade squatted, sucked in his breath like he was about to reveal something almost too horrific to deal with. He shook his head back and forth.

"Oda MacFarland's cross."

Oda MacFarland! Lord, deliver me! At last month's Senior Dinner I'm saying grace, using the microphone, when Oda shouts, "Speak up, we can't hear you."

Velma Atwater walks over to him and shouts in his ear, "YOU can't hear."

"Don't interrupt the prayer!" Oda shouts at her.

"You already did!" she yells. By now pandemonium has broken out, half of the group taking Velma's side, half defending Oda.

"Amen." I got out of there as fast as I could.

Now Wade was staring into my eyes, his own glistening with tears. "Oda donated this. Made it himself in his younger years. I understand it hung in the sanctuary before the organ was installed up front. Act of love, it was. Shouldn't be hidden away." Like I'm responsible for this grave oversight.

"What do you propose?"

He grasped a metal end. "What do I propose? What do I propose? We've got to hang this back up."

I start to type the article: *For three years I've been blessed to minister to the elderly.* A bold lie. I'm stuck in a dying church. "Give ministry one more try," that's what Marsha said. "Accept the call."

Ministering to the elderly, while it has its challenges, certainly has its rewards as well. What rewards? A broken leg, that's what. Stay off it for three weeks the surgeon ordered.

So later I went back in the room and gave the cross another look. Wade had rearranged some of the clutter, stacked more junk on the pews, moved aside the plastic flowers and old

16

hymnals. Now the cross lay there fully exposed, three giant aluminum tubes welded together. You don't have to be a certified art critic to see that it's the work of a hack with a welding torch.

Good Lord. Wade had already formed an ad hoc committee. Three women, the very ones who're always complaining about Oda. For some weird reason a stroke of compassion suddenly overtook them. Stroke. Why can't the geezer just have a stroke and keel over? It would save us all some grief. I'm the one who's gonna have a stroke, all the pressure I've been living with. I feel my blood pressure spiking right now.

This committee, three women plus Wade, they invaded my office, stood before me, arms crossed. And started reminiscing. About the days when Happy Corner had a dynamic minister. Which I obviously am not. Back when some woman named Betty made the best hot cross buns you ever tasted. And some man named—I forget his name—he'd roast a hog in a pit and organize a picnic. For the whole church. The good old days.

The contributions of older members often go unrecognized. It is important to use their talents.

"Poor Oda," Elsie Kirkakoff said. "He's never complained. His work discarded like a piece of junk."

Which it is: a piece of junk.

Estella Hathaway: "Had to have hurt his feelings."

"We've got to hang it up. Otherwise, he'll go to his grave thinking we didn't value his gift."

I became a referee. The three women constantly invading my office versus the few discerning individuals who recognize the cross is ugly. Velma Atwater went so far as to threaten to take her membership elsewhere if the cross goes up. But I know where my bread is buttered. The Hathaways are our biggest contributors.

Older members, educated their whole lives to tithe, can be depended on to continue supporting the church financially.

Marsha spread plastic sheets and newspapers on the parsonage living room floor. Wade and I carried the monstros-

17

ity over. Ten feet tall. Ten feet! You had to step over it to go from the front door to the kitchen, to the bathroom, to the bedrooms. Can this cross be saved? Can accord among the members of Happy Corner be saved? Can democracy be saved? Can the planet Earth be saved? Can the contract between Reverend Bill Benedict and the Happy Corner Baptist Church be saved?

SO I'M SITTING there on the living room floor thinking maybe I should have been a carpenter or a painter or a lumberjack. For a long time I wanted to be a dress designer. Up through junior high I'd use my mother's left-over fabric pieces to make clothes for my little sister's dolls. I told my high school counselor, who immediately advised me to find another hobby. Otherwise, people would start saying I was a—don't go there, Bill.

Lemon juice and baking soda. Over the entire surface. Top to bottom. Tip of one arm to the tip of the other. Soak the rag, scrub. Soak the rag, scrub. Soak the rag . . . Physical effort lets a guy's mind wander to things he hasn't thought about in a long time. Soak the rag, scrub. Soak the rag, scrub. Soak the rag.

"If you cannot preach like Peter," I sing. "If you cannot pray like Paul." They want a Norman Vincent Peale, a Billy Graham. Just because Happy Corner was once a prominent church they think one man, me—I should be able to bring the past back. Soak the rag, rub. RUB, I tell you! RUB! I have forty-five bosses. Who can please forty-five bosses? Visit the shut-ins. Develop a youth group. Bring back some of the members who left. How? With my charisma? Which doesn't exist?

Soak the rag. Scrub. Soak the rag. Scrub. Scrub. SCRUB!

I could have . . . I could have been a geologist. No, I wasn't all that good in science. The problem right there. I lacked direction. So when Marsha pressured me—no, be honest, man, she encouraged. If she says, you can do it, then I think, yeah, I can. Face it, Bill you can't. You're a failure. She won't tell you that, but it's the truth.

Sandpaper with a fine grit. Start at the top. I could quit, find another job. What kind of job do you think you're qualified for? I could be a social worker. Left arm of the cross. Rub with sandpaper. Rub with sandpaper. Gently. Human resources, I'd be good at that. Getting rid of the oxidation, bringing a shine. Sanding the seams.

I've been faithful. To the church, to Marsha. Willamina Hughes. Eve with the apple, that woman. We worked well together. Flirted even. There've been other women who thought I have a certain appeal about me. But did I stray? Never. Maybe I should have.

Gently now, rub gently, like I'm caressing a woman's legs. Not Marsha's. Hers aren't bad though. She's okay in bed. Unenthusiastic but okay. Women I see out on the street with their ample breasts, necklines showing cleavage. Gently, rub gently.

I lean back on my haunches. The cross catches a stream of sunlight breaking through the window. It gleams. I start singing again. "Sometimes I feel discouraged and think my work's in vain, but then the Holy Spirit revives my soul again. There is a balm . . ."

WADE KIRKAKOFF'S DECISION, not mine. The symbolism and all, he said. Resurrection on Easter Sunday, the cross without a body. The resurrection of Oda's cross, hanging to the right of the pulpit, where the slotted hymn board has hung since God knows when. The two of us carried the cross, light in weight but bulky, from the parsonage floor into the sanctuary. While we stood on ladders and supported it, women on the committee supervised.

"The bottom needs to go a little to the right."

"Now to the left."

"Tweak the right arm a little. Down. That's it. That's it."

Nearly an hour passed before everyone was satisfied.

Easter Sunday I'm sitting up there on the podium. In my navy-blue suit. The yellow tie Marsha says I should wear because Easter marks the beginning of spring, and spring is the time of resurrection, the plants and trees starting to bloom and all, and besides she has a new yellow dress, so we'll complement each other.

I looked out over the scattered faithful. Lilies lined the edge of the pulpit; baskets of purple pansies adorned the windowsills. To my right—out of my line of vision but I knew it loomed: the cross. Three aluminum pipes welded together.

I heard him before I saw him: Oda MacFarland. Telling somebody in the narthex to speak up. He entered the sanctuary, cane in his right hand, leaning heavily on the arm of his granddaughter, Jennifer. Made his way toward his usual place in the fifth row. He was almost there when he looked up, stopped abruptly, then squinted. Stretched his neck forward then back like a turkey.

He pointed his cane. "Who in the blazes put that monstrosity up there?"

He was yelling. A cluster of women rushed toward him, shouting above Stella's prelude that the cross is a lovely work of art and a valued gift to the church.

"I may be deaf but I'm not blind. That thing's ugly as sin." He was still yelling.

Lord, deliver me. I wanted to duck behind the pulpit. No, Bill, you're in charge here. Do something. But I could only sit there staring at the gaggle of women yelling in Oda's face, hovering so close—how could the man even breathe? He started swinging his cane with more force than an eighty-nine-year-old should be capable of. Little Herbie Hollinger, seated nearby, ducked under the pew. The women retreated. Except for Velma Atwater. She and Oda stood in the center aisle, eye to eye, both with a grip on his cane, pivoting like boxers, grunting. But Oda held on firmly. Ann, her Easter suit all askew, her hat on the floor near Oda's feet, finally withdrew breathless from the ring. But Oda kept swinging his cane.

"Ugly as sin. Ugly as sin."

I took a deep breath and stepped down from the podium. On TV I've seen police approach a man or woman, trying to coax them to give up their gun or not jump off a building. I took calm strides toward Oda, maintained a soothing tone, yet I had to speak loud enough for him to hear.

"Now, now, Mr. MacFarland. No need to get upset. We're in church and it's Easter Sunday. Jesus has risen. Let's go to our seat and celebrate our risen Lord."

Oda swung his cane.

"Goddamn! You old fool!" I grabbed my shin and fell to the floor. "Give me air, give me air!" I yelled to the biddies who hovered over me. Hands to the floor, I pushed myself up.

As if nothing happened, Oda reached for his granddaughter's arm and went to his usual seat. As if nothing happened, I limped up the steps and plopped down on the chair. The show must go on. The drama of an escaped body. The Melrose Family sang "Up From the Grave He Arose."

Standing before the worshippers, my leg throbbing in pain, I preached on "What Resurrection Means Today," which bored me as much as it probably bored everyone present.

Afterlife

IF GIVEN THE OPTION Vera Petry would decline her fifteen minutes of fame. But there's her name on the front page of *The Gazette*. In small print, but there all the same, in a column alongside Wally's picture and the headline, "Area man wants others to learn from his experience."

Seems Wally *does* want his fifteen minutes. Not that it should matter to her what kind of fool he makes of himself. Now he's gone and dragged her into his pathetic narrative.

Vera, Vera, who bothers to read this free weekly anymore?

Sold to a Black family, what had been her and Wally's home only seven blocks from here. He was convinced they had to move out to the suburbs before "them coloreds take over every f-ing thing." Even though cramped—what with five kids—their modest bungalow had a warmth that enveloped Vera and helped her cope.

Who could have predicted that young professionals would come to see the benefits of urban living? Sturdy stone houses were bought cheap and transformed into elegant homes. The neighborhood changed from Black to white, only this time family incomes have six figures, seven even. The last she heard that little house she and Wally owned went for three-quarters of a million dollars. Three-quarters of a million!

Vera gets up from the kitchen table and puts her cereal bowl in the dishwasher. She pauses in front of the narrow window over the sink. Two stories below, pedestrians walk into the March wind, heads bent, hands clutching coat collars. Up and down the street specialty shops accommodate families wanting chef-prepared dishes to carry home at the end of the day. Coffee shops charge five dollars for a cup of coffee and boutiques sell purses for four hundred dollars.

23

Two svelte young women in sweatpants jog along the edge of the sidewalk. Will they get coffee afterward? Sit in an intimate booth and talk about—what do women that age talk about?

Wally always interfered with her friendships. He criticized women she liked, saying they were stupid or ugly or bad mothers or bad—the possibilities of *bad* were endless. And what, he demanded to know, made her think she had time for socializing when the house was a mess? When the kids needed more supervision? When he needed her? She never understood what he needed her for. Except dinner on the table. And sex. On demand.

During the early years of their marriage, the Happy Corner Church was her refuge. She'd drop the kids off early at Children's Worship then meet Annie in the church kitchen down in the basement. Unless a Sunday luncheon was on the calendar, the two visited in quiet, sometimes skipping the worship service altogether. Soon after Wally insisted on moving to the suburbs, Annie was killed in a car accident. To this day, Vera misses her dear friend.

Now she has two new friends, Barbara and Henrietta. The three don't much discuss their pasts. All Barbara and Henrietta know is that Vera's husband is in prison. *Was* in prison, until three days ago. They both recently retired from careers that gave them an identity, Barbara as a school librarian, Henrietta as a social worker. Vera's identity? She still struggles to consider herself anything other than wife, mother, cook, vacuumer, toilet bowl scrubber.

No, you're a different woman now. A strong woman.

She pours another cup of coffee, inhales the pleasant pungent aroma, carries the newspaper back into the living room. Out of habit she counts the steps from the kitchen into the beige carpeted living room. One, two, three . . . up to twelve. Until Wally's release she's felt secure in her condo on the third floor, two locked doors between her and the outside. With Wally free though . . .

Her space. She moved back to the neighborhood after the divorce settlement, into the old high school converted to luxury condos. Hers isn't enormous like most of the other units. Certainly not like the penthouse owned by a mysterious person no one in the building has ever met, but whose representative attends all the condo meetings: a woman in her fifties who carries a satchel with a tapestry of Elvis's face on the flap.

Vera has two bedrooms, the master suite with a spa bathtub and a closet bigger than Wally's prison cell probably was. Her condo has the warm tones she prefers: ecru walls, sofa and recliner upholstered in rust-toned velour, drapes of a petite floral print. Her living room window offers a view of the park, where on warm days she sometimes sits on a bench near the statue of Edgar Allen Poe.

Vera can walk to practically everything she needs. Except church. The neighborhood around it has changed since her father walked her up the center aisle to "Here Comes the Bride." She feels a little uneasy when she drives there. Not the fifteen-minute drive itself but the challenge of finding a parking place along the street and having to walk past boarded up houses and vacant lots strewn with litter.

Lifting Puffy from the velour recliner, Vera sits, stares at Wally's picture in the newspaper. Puffy curls next to her, purring as she rubs his luxuriant white fur.

Puffy, her final line of defense against Wally.

The spectacle he's made of their life. First the shock of the kidnapping, followed by the trial's publicity and his incarceration. Now a newspaper interview. Acting contrite when she knows good and well he isn't. His rags-to-riches saga soaked up by a perky young reporter who's probably no older than his own children. He's always had that way about him. Not charm. No one would describe Wally as charming. It's his ability to convince. His fake sincerity.

"His wife's determination to get a divorce drove him to such drastic measures, Petry states. He insists that he still does not understand why she wanted to end their marriage."

Of course, he doesn't understand. That's why she wanted the divorce, because he didn't understand how a man should treat his wife.

Five babies born one right after the other. Using fabric from others' cast-off clothes, Vera sewed dresses for the girls, shirts for the boys. She had ten recipes for canned tuna, as many for Spam. Vera was the one who took Lizzy to the emergency room, physically carried the ten-year-old fifteen blocks. Vera who made the burial arrangements. Who had to subdue her own grief to hold the family together.

The life Vera reads about holds little resemblance to the real one. To his credit Wally worked hard to provide for the family, like the article says. He started his own construction company, working fifteen-hour days to make it grow. He claimed to be doing it for the family, but after a while it was obvious he wanted money for money's sake. Then more money. Then even more. Until he was driving a big Cadillac, wearing gold chains around his neck and sporting a diamond ring on his pinkie.

"What do you think I'm made of?" he bellowed when she came home with a dress she'd bought for thirty-five dollars on a clearance rack. "An f-ing gold mine?" He made her return it.

He promised she could help design their new house in the suburbs. She wanted a cozy home with a fireplace and an eat-in kitchen. He built a monstrosity with the gosh-awfullest pillars on a portico and fancy wrought-iron trim everywhere. He put in a circular drive with an ornate Italian fountain in the middle, and a four-car garage.

Seven years. Seven years since Vera decided she deserved better and finally found the courage to demand a divorce. Even with the legal bond of marriage broken, it took a while to drown out Wally's mocking tone, his condescension.

You're a different woman now. A strong woman.

She gets affirmation from reading at the nearby elementary school, embracing her grandmotherly role, holding sweet runny-nosed five-year-olds on her lap, taking on the voices of growling wolves and squeaking mice. She sings in a community chorus and takes piano lessons.

Now Wally's been released. She tosses the newspaper on the floor. Too many memories. Too many memories.

It's almost time for *The View*. A needed distraction. Vera anticipates a guest author or a woman telling how she found healing. Yesterday it was by scaling El Capitan. She picks up the remote. Clicks. Takes a sip of coffee from the mug Robbie gave her, "World's Best Mom" in big red letters.

Shit!

There's Wally on the local news, standing in front of the camera, acting like he's on the verge of tears. His third day out of prison, already playing the victim. What a faker. Making that little blonde gal who covers the emotional stories feel sorry for him.

He's six years older than the last time she saw him. The thick black hair he always took pride in is thinning and has some gray in it. A paunch hangs over his belt. But he has the same diffident smile and crows feet next to his eyes. He's using his public voice, the velvety one she had no access to.

"What do you wish you could tell young husbands?" the woman asks.

"To make time for the family, not to get so fired up about providin' that they give up spendin' time with the people they love most."

It took six years in prison to learn that? Bringing the remote down as if it's a gavel, Vera clicks the television into darkness.

Spend more time with the family? The year he decided to do just that. A vacation, he said, they should take a real vacation. To Vegas, where Wally hung out in the casino while she kept the kids entertained. Him stumbling into the room at three in the morning, cursing that if she'd stayed by his side she would have brought him luck.

Vera gets up, giving the chair back to Puffy, who yawns and stretches his paws. Counting the twelve steps back to the kitchen, she drops the newspaper on the recycling pile under the breakfast bar, glances around her kitchen with satisfaction. The Sub-zero refrigerator and maple cupboards. An expensive condo with everything she wanted. Financed by the settlement. The paper mentions that too, how Wally thinks it was an unfair amount. *Not one cent more than I deserve, given all I put up with over the years.*

AT NOON VERA WALKS TO the Post Office to return a sweater she ordered through a catalog. The cut's unflattering, makes her look big in the hips. When she comes out, there's Wally leaning against the blue mailbox, fingertips of one hand tapping the white eagle, the other hand poking at his gums with a toothpick. He wears a Baltimore Orioles baseball cap and a pair of faded jeans.

"Hi there, Vera," he says, falling into step as if they're still married. Vera says nothing. Instead of stopping by the drugstore to pick up a prescription, as planned, she heads directly home.

"Aren't you going to invite me in?" he asks as her key unlocks the front door of the building.

"No!"

Should have done that back in '70. Shut the door in his face and never spoken to him again. That damned way of his, those words of flattery after she spilled a tiny pitcher of cream on his clean Army uniform. Her boss, acting all patriotic, gave him his breakfast free then took it out of her wages. If she hadn't spilled the cream, Wally would have gone to another restaurant the next time he was hungry. Instead, he returned the following three mornings and stayed until the end of her shift, told her over and over how pretty she was. A real compliment to a girl who didn't think she was at all pretty.

"Aren't you going to invite me in?" Wally asked Vera three days later when he walked her home from work. A month after that, a week after her eighteenth birthday and the day before he was shipped overseas, they were married in the Happy Corner Baptist Church.

You're a different woman now. A strong woman.

"YOU'RE LOOKING GOOD, Vera." Wally stands in the middle of the sidewalk, right outside Jentzens' Drug Store.

She says nothing. Yes, she looks good because she's lost twenty pounds, and Lanie colored her hair auburn and cut it differently. Lanie said it's the latest style, but Vera sees a resemblance to the shag from the seventies and hopes the double-knit suit in her basement storage space will come back in style too.

A breeze from the south, relief from the cold spell they've been having, brushes her face. She was thinking about strolling over to Memorial Park, sit awhile in the sun across from Edgar Allen Poe. But Wally will follow along, and she doesn't want to risk being seen with him.

Too late. Here comes Mary Beth Reece, walking in their direction. Mary Beth. with a social antenna like the Eiffel Tower and a Mammoth Cave mouth, who stops to say hello, flashes that super-friendly smile of hers, and asks, "Where you living now, Wally?" Like she's hoping to pass along word that Wally and Vera are cohabitating. A former member of the Happy Corner Church, she's kept her connections.

Sure enough, on Sunday Althena Melrose approaches Vera in the church vestibule. Says in that syrupy voice of hers that she heard Vera and Wally are back together, that people have seen them walking down the street. *People* has to mean Mary Beth. "We're all cheering for you," Althena tells Vera, patting her on the arm.

Unlike other members, Vera likes the shrunken size of the congregation, the small flock of worshippers who've remained despite the neighborhood changing. The service is calmer and there aren't so many people to greet. She occupies the middle of a pew in the fourth row from the back. In front of her Stephanie Byers sits with her young daughter, who's coloring the bulletin with a purple crayon. The little girl's pink tutu and black leotards take Vera back to arguments with Lila about what to wear to church. In hindsight she wishes she'd been more relaxed. At the organ Stella stumbles through the prelude, which sounds a little like "Jesu, Joy of Man's Desiring." Up on the pulpit Pastor Bill sits, head bowed—in prayer, Vera assumes.

Good God, there's Wally, eight rows in front of her. He used to say he wouldn't go anywhere he couldn't wear jeans and a hard hat. He seems to have changed his mind. He's wearing a suit.

This morning Pastor Bill preaches on the sanctity of the family while his wife, Marsha, sits near the front.

"How easy it is to dissolve the bonds of marriage," Pastor Bill says.

Is Marsha happy? Vera wonders, recalling the exact day she realized she wasn't. The three older children had all moved out—Brian to live with a girlfriend; Robbie to rent an apartment with two friends; Lila to New York, hoping to establish an acting career. Only Kelly remained at home. Wally, in a fit of anger—something so minor Vera doesn't remember the reason—threw a glass against the refrigerator and stomped out of the room. Vera fetched a broom and dustpan. Instead of sweeping up the glass, though, she sat on the floor, picked up a shard, studied the way it reflected the kitchen light, the way it came to a point. She pressed the point against her wrist. A drop of blood formed a small puddle. Pressing harder, she watched the crimson liquid trickle onto her white blouse.

Why did she pull the shard away, stand, and take a tissue from the box? Because she finally understood that she deserved better.

People need to *work* on their relationship, Pastor Bill reminds the congregation. What God hath joined together . . . Wally turns around and winks at Vera.

VERA TREASURES HER FREEDOM. Freedom to sip a morning cup of coffee in peace, then drive to the mall or to the museum. Or go read to preschoolers. She's free to take piano lessons and practice when she wishes.

Since fifth grade, when the music teacher performed "Moonlight Sonata" for the school assembly, Vera dreamed of having a piano. When she told Wally how much she wanted one—they were, after all, on sound financial footing—he mocked the notion. A thirty-five-year-old woman starting lessons? There were more important ways to spend her time and his money.

After lunch she sits on the piano bench, practicing "Für Elise," which she'll perform at the recital. One, two, three, one, two, three. The beauty of the piece brings tears to her eyes.

The telephone interrupts her practicing. It's Kelly, who calls several times a week, her words always interrupted by crying spells. She frets about her studies and about whether her lit teacher likes her and about what her roommate thinks of her and about the pimple on her forehead. Kelly, the child who's paid the highest emotional cost.

She had been pleased when her father picked her up from school, excited about the trip the two of them were going on. Wally hadn't thought his actions through to their logical conclusion: that when Kelly didn't disembark from the school bus, when no one knew where she was—it seemed not to have occurred to Wally that Vera would call the police. For five days she waited frantically by the phone, until the police found the two, Kelly distraught, out in Utah. What Wally had intended as revenge for the divorce, ended up landing him in prison for kidnapping.

Some days she blames him for their dysfunctional family. Other days she blames herself for having been the pathetic enabler. That's the word Lucy has used in therapy sessions: enabler.

You're a different woman now. A strong woman.

HER SHOPPING BASKET contains a quart of milk, a small plastic container of Tide, two rolls of toilet paper, a small bag of coconut cookies. Plus seven frozen Weight Watcher dinners. Rounding the corner at the end of the aisle, her mind focused on which line will be quickest, she nearly runs into Wally, carrying two six-packs.

Her head turned away is meant to signal her intention to ignore his presence. He steps in front of her. "Hello, Vera," he says, not in the loving tone of someone who wants his wife back but in a menacing voice, as if she'd better say hello too. Instead, she puts the grocery basket in front of her and bulldozes past her ex-husband, who is nearly twice her weight. A lane has just opened. Vera places the groceries onto the black belt.

Moments later she pushes her two-wheeled shopping cart along the sidewalk, taking rapid steps while Wally's long strides persist beside her.

"Want me to help you take those upstairs?" he asks when they come to her building.

"No."

She unlocks the main door, opens it only enough to place the bag of groceries inside, folds her cart, and squeezes her body through a narrow space. She shuts the door behind her.

Inside, she leans against the locked door and whistles a sigh of relief. He could have forced his way in, would have in his younger years when he thought he had a right to her.

That's why she's got Puffy.

She imagines Wally inhaling Puffy's dander, gasping for air. Vera would call the paramedics right away. She doesn't want him dying on her beige living room carpeting.

TWO WEEKS HAVE PASSED since the newspaper article. Fourteen days of running into Wally every time she ventures from the condo. At the music store, at the library. She considers calling the police and accusing him of stalking. But doesn't.

People she hasn't seen for years, former neighbors from the suburbs, have been calling to talk about Wally. "He's hurtin' real bad." "The man's paid for his crime." All of them expressing hope that she and Wally will reconcile.

ON A RAINY FRIDAY afternoon Pastor Bill pays a visit. He's a good man, Vera thinks, not a dynamic preacher, but she's seen him affectionately pull Marsha to his side and smile into her face. Vera offers him coffee and cookies from the bag she bought at the grocery. The Lord has laid something on his heart, he says. Wally isn't doing very well without her, and Pastor Bill prays she'll reconsider.

Reconsider what? she wants to know.

You know, getting back together.

Because he isn't doing very well without me?

It's hard for a man who relied on a wife for so long to suddenly get by on his own.

Hard on a man, huh? He got along fine without me in prison.

Remember what our Lord told Peter: to forgive seventy times seven. It's time you forgive Wally. Besides, these are the golden years, a time when a man and a woman are meant to be companions for each other.

She offers Pastor Bill more cookies.

Golden years. Yes, they'll be golden years for her. Alone. But she says nothing of that to the pastor, just keeps offering him more cookies and watching his mouth move, amused by the deep concern in his hazel eyes.

When the cookies are gone, he leaves, telling Vera to think it over—prayerfully. She will, she promises, and walks him to the elevator.

She goes into her bedroom and pulls the draperies. Slowly, deliberately, she peels off her clothes, starting with the yellow sweater and gray slacks, ending with her panties and bra.

Standing in front of the wide dresser mirror, she runs her fingers up and down her arms then brings them to her shoulders, where they trace the grooves dug by years of wearing bras.

She reaches down and rubs her thighs, once muscular, now fleshy and marbled.

She wishes for scars on her body. If she had visible scars, people wouldn't be so quick to think she ought to take Wally back. But the scars are inside, so nobody seems to notice. Not even the kidnapping convinced them, the terror she lived with while police searched, Kelly's confusion when her daddy drove at breakneck speed across the Midwest, his refusal to let her call Vera.

Arms to her sides, she stares into the mirror. Wally assumed it belonged to him, her body. God, what will it take for people to recognize that a woman's body isn't anyone's possession but her own?

Without putting her clothes back on, Vera walks back into the living room and sits down in her recliner. "Here, kitty," she softly calls as Puffy peers around the corner. Puffy stares for a moment, then turns and walks away.

Oh, cat, what an inspiration you are.

Paradise Unraveled, Part I

A fairer person lost not Heaven; he seemed
For dignity composed and high exploit;
But all was false and hollow; though his tongue
Dropped manna, and made the worst appear
The better reason.
Paradise Lost, Book II, lines 110-114

YEARS HAD PASSED since anyone new had attended Happy Corner. But there they were one Sunday morning: Stan Acheron, Senior, a broad-shouldered, middle-aged man with a good head of black hair, and a petite redhead named Lucy, whose strong soprano voice, when singing "The Doxology," filled the sanctuary. Two teenagers: Stan Junior, with a swagger to his stride, and a daughter, Evelyn, dressed in black leather and multiply pierced. During coffee hour after the service, Stan Senior and Lucy mingled comfortably and expressed enthusiasm over becoming members. The teens mainly gazed at their feet.

Later, answers to where the family came from depended on who you asked. From Oregon, Roland Martin thought. From Missouri, Tom Hamilton said. Elsie Kirkakoff was sure they had moved from Arizona.

Stan had taken a job teaching ethics at the college, out in the suburbs. Lucy taught private piano and organ lessons there too. "We want to worship where our skills are useful," they repeated often during the first weeks of attendance. Stan Senior volunteered to serve as the adult advisor to the youth group. "They are the church leaders of tomorrow," he said.

THOSE MOST KNOWLEDGEABLE about the egresses and ingresses at Happy Corner Baptist Church could only account for the need for seven keys, yet Wade Kirkakoff, longtime chairman of the Buildings and Grounds Committee, carried thirty on the metal ring attached to his belt. Like miniature bell clappers, the keys hitting against each other announced Wade's approach.

In his late sixties, Wade had a widening bald spot encircled by light brown hair. Over the years his waistline had expanded to such a degree that his wife, Elsie, couldn't begin to reach around it anymore. Tiny ruptured blood vessels spread like spiderwebs across his broad nose, crooked from a childhood accident. He seldom smiled, not because he wasn't good-natured, but because he was self-conscious about a missing tooth just behind his upper-right canine.

Everyone at the church held Wade in high regard. People appreciated his fastidiousness about the church building and grounds. Not only did he make sure that everything with moving parts was in tiptop condition, but he made certain that—as he remembered his grandmother saying—there was a place for everything and everything was in its place.

Elsie, too, was a pillar of the church. A tall, slender woman, she had an angular bone structure with sharp elbows that only a few ever saw nudge Wade in the ribs. As self-appointed church librarian, she welcomed donations of books and created bulletin boards that encouraged members to read. Every Sunday she opened the church library at exactly five minutes after the end of the service. Though seldom more than three children waited, she insisted that they line up and enter in an orderly fashion. At her tidy desk she then lifted the stamp, which she'd set earlier in the morning for the next due date. Elsie took pride in how organized the library was and insisted that instead of reshelving books, people put them on the cart next to her desk so that she could put them where they belonged.

Both Wade and Elsie were equally fastidious about their appearance. Wade's navy-blue suit was shiny from its many pressings, and he polished his black shoes every Saturday night. Elsie dressed neatly and made sure that every gray hair on her head was in its proper place.

When Pastor Bill had first come to Happy Corner, he set a goal of visiting in the home of each member family. "A house says a lot about the people who live in it," he told Marsha, who lowered her chin and asked "What does ours say?" In truth it was a point of contention, as Marsha frequently had to remind Bill to pick his socks and underwear up off the floor.

Pastor Bill had spent an hour in the brick ranch house of Stella and Tom Hamilton, eating Stella's Luscious Lemon Loaf at the dining room table, listening to Tom say how much he admired Stella's willingness to share the gift of music. At the home of Dallas and Margaret Hines, the TV stayed tuned to a quiz show while Margaret served peach pie with a big dip of vanilla ice cream on the side. Several times Margaret tried to mellow Dallas's bombastic way with "Now Dallas, I know you don't mean that the way it sounds."

Yet Bill had never been in Wade and Elsie's house. Several times he'd tried to make an appointment to visit them. Elsie's sister was coming. Wade had a rheumatologist appointment. "Well, we're going to be at the church that afternoon anyway. Why don't the three of us just visit in your office?"

AFTER CHURCH ONE Sunday Lucy called Wade aside. "Who does the church hire for plumbing? We need a new sink and vanity in our upstairs bathroom."

"I handle all the repairs." He went on to explain that Lucy's project would be a simple task and he'd be glad to do it. "I get a lot of pleasure out of helping friends."

The following Wednesday, at Wilmot's Kitchen and Bath Supply, Wade was aware of other customers looking at them as they walked among the floor samples. Lucy with her flaming red hair and shapely figure and—*What is she doing with a lump of a man like that?* they probably wondered. He straightened his posture.

Later, as he installed the new sink and vanity, the drip of the shower and a gurgle coming from the toilet caught his attention. He replaced the showerhead and the toilet flush valve, all the while humming, sometimes whistling through his teeth, other times singing loud enough that Lucy heard him.

"What a good voice you have." Which surprised Wade, for he'd never thought of himself as musical. "You know, Happy Corner needs a choir. Does Elsie sing too?"

"Yes, I guess you could say she does. You know, we used to have one, but our best voices left, moved out to the suburbs."

"Well, Happy Corner's music program is going to rise from the dead."

Soon there was a choir, six people at first, then eight. Then twelve, after two couples visited the church and were impressed by the music. It didn't seem right, Lucy said, for the choir to sing from the loft in the back of the sanctuary, where it couldn't be seen. At her request Wade moved the chairs onto the dais in front, near the organ.

Choir members couldn't help but comment on how, when Lucy directed, her whole being coaxed them to sing from their diaphragms and create resonating space with their wide-open mouths. Strength was in her arms, and energy pulsated through-out her body. *It just goes to show that if you've got a topnotch musician leading you,* people said, *just about anybody can make a joyful noise unto the Lord.*

It was as if by telling them they could sing, Lucy was able to conjure the music that had been sequestered in their souls. Sometimes she had Stella move aside and took it upon herself to play the organ with her right hand while directing with her left. Or she stood behind a music rack, moving her whole body in rhythm to the song, using large movements in which her hands reached out and pulled, pulled until she'd dislodged all inhibitions and drawn them into herself.

Pastor Bill noticed that with the choir up front, filling the air with harmony, and with Lucy pumping her energy into the service, his sermons were improving.

As often happens when individuals strive together, the choir was becoming a close-knit group, for basses recognized how the contrast with sopranos enhanced their timbre, and altos knew that sweet tenor tones made their own voices all the richer. Every Wednesday night after rehearsal, even when January temperatures dipped into single digits, everyone met at Greiner's Old Fashioned Ice Cream. There was always a rush to the order window to see who would treat Lucy. Her favorite flavor, everyone knew, was Heavenly Hash.

To be by Lucy's side was to engage in a conviviality that those at the opposite end of the table envied. Everyone near her was joking and telling funny stories about events that had either happened to them or to someone they knew or which they remembered reading somewhere. Better, though, to be out of earshot than not present at all.

When the annual council meeting came along, Lucy was elected to the church board.

LOWER AND LOWER Pastor Bill's head drooped until it came to a restful stop on his desk. A trickle of saliva escaping the corner of his mouth created a small puddle on his sermon manuscript. He was awakened by a hand on his shoulder, a gentle touch which at first he thought was real, then a dream, but which ended up being real after all. It was Lucy's hand softly gripping his shoulder. With a jerk he lifted his head and immediately wiped the moisture from both his mouth and the piece of paper.

"Come here, I want to show you something." She led him down the hallway, then, standing behind him, her hands covering his eyes, she gently pushed him into the room.

"Ta-da!" Instead of the tables for the upcoming board meeting being arranged in a large square with a hole in the middle, they were connected lengthwise, metal folding chairs on both sides. Bill was startled to see at opposite ends of the adjoining tables the two large pulpit chairs he'd moved to the storage area behind the chancel. With their high backs, red cushioned seats, and elaborate carvings, they had looked too much like thrones to suit him.

"I found them hiding in that grungy storage room," Lucy told him, her eyes glistening with enthusiasm. "Wade cleaned them up. I'll sit down there," she pointed toward one end of the table, "and you'll sit here."

Bill stammered, "Uh,uh,uh, bu-bu-but, it makes us look like king and queen."

"Yes," she said, apparently pleased that he'd caught on. "But it conveys the message that you and I are in charge."

"I've been meaning to bring that up. Let's you and I have a talk." She motioned for him to sit in what she'd designated to be his chair. Then she stepped back and pretending to hold a camera to her eye, said "click." She sat on the folding chair to his right.

"I think," she said, "that while your ideas about everything being democratic are admirable, they're not really practical. An organization, be it a church, a club, whatever, needs strong leadership in order to move forward. Why, in the short time I've been a member here, I've seen what a gifted man you are, and Bill, it's like you put your light under a bushel. You're so conscientious about letting everyone have a voice that things are often chaotic, and the church doesn't get the full benefit of your abilities." She placed a hand on his arm and peered intently into his eyes. "You could be doing so much more for this church if you'd only quit trying to keep such a tight hold on your own impulses. You need to let go, be who you really are. That person, I'm convinced, is an outstanding leader who could really move this church forward."

Lucy leaned back in the chair and gave him a satisfied closed-mouth smile.

"Well," he said, "let's see how the board reacts to this arrangement."

"Bill, you miss my point. You can't let the board decide. To be a strong leader, you yourself must decide. Here."

The way her hands pressed his shoulders back then placed his arms on the chair's wooden armrests was both disconcerting and exciting. It was precisely because her touch was so exciting that he found it disconcerting.

"It's a perfect fit," she said.

BILL WASN'T ONE to fantasize about undressing women as much as about dressing them. Marsha never went shopping for clothes without taking him along, and unlike most men, he would, at Christmas, present her with a most becoming ensemble he himself had selected.

Today he couldn't help but notice how stunning Lucy looked, her red hair contrasting with the bright yellow matching sweater and pants she wore. It occurred to him that she would be an interesting woman to design clothes for, not because of her looks, though she was pretty, but because of the élan with which she carried herself.

"Isn't it incredible," she said, "how many people have turned out for the choir? And don't the voices blend well? You know, in just this short time our family's come to love it here at Happy Corner. Oh, and Bill, your sermons! They're filled with so much wisdom. Every Sunday I can hardly wait to hear what you're going to say."

"Yes, ours is a special group of people. And I want you to know—" Here he made sure his voice took on an extra note of sincerity— "I want you to know how much I value what you've already done for the church. You know, a good choir sets the tone of a worship service." He chuckled lightly. "Which in turn makes me look good."

"I have a concern, though." Her unease could be seen in the sudden droop of her mouth. "That's why I'm here this afternoon. Maybe you could help me figure out what to do."

She leaned forward. "God knows, Stella's heart is in the right place, but—well with your keen ear, Bill, you've got to notice that, well, she really doesn't have the musical background to be playing that magnificent instrument. You know how hard the choir's working. I can't believe they've only been singing together a little over two months. But Stella, bless her heart, she stumbles along and, and—to be honest, Bill, the quality of her playing . . . Oh, I just don't know how to say it kindly—it detracts from the choir's excellence."

Worry lines crossed her forehead, her mouth was puckered. "I'm also worried about how this affects her. You can just see all the tension that's been building up in her. When I talk with her right before the worship service, I want to put my arms around her and say, 'Stella, dear Stella, relax, relax.' Playing the organ every Sunday—why, you know how hard she practices. All that pressure can't be good for her health. Did you notice how last Sunday, at the end of the offertory, she put her hand to her heart?"

Bill hadn't noticed. He certainly didn't want Stella to feel like playing the organ was a burden, and heaven forbid that her health would be ruined by this responsibility.

"Do you have any idea what we can do for her?" he asked.

"One possibility—it came to me just this morning, in fact—my idea is that we could offer her a sabbatical. Maybe a two- or three-month leave."

"But how could we manage without her?"

"I wouldn't mind substituting for a few months. I really do believe the poor woman needs a break."

With that matter settled, the two of them, Bill and Lucy, sat by the office window and talked. At first about the history of the church: the Farley Buggy Company and what a magnificent organ the Byron Keeling Family had donated, and how the neighborhood had changed. They talked until outside the window, darkness had replaced daylight.

LUCY WAS LATER than usual, and Bill came close to confessing to himself that he hadn't been able to get anything done for the past hour while his mind anticipated her bounding into the room with her limitless energy, but then calmly sitting with him by the window. What a remarkable blend of energy and empathy.

"I've been thinking," Lucy said when she finally arrived, "people in the church are all so busy. There's a meeting for this and one for that, not to mention all the other activities they're involved in. If we could cut out a meeting we'd be doing everyone a favor."

"What do you have in mind?"

"Since you and I talk nearly every day anyway, and since much of our talk is about the worship service, it seems redundant to have a Worship Committee. You know what it does to aesthetics every time someone who lacks understanding starts tampering with what you and I envision." She paused, her eyes brimming with admiration. "You have such an eye and ear for beauty. If just the two of us work on a service—why the way we energize each other—Bill, we can't create a work of art by group consensus."

He certainly wouldn't mind cutting out a meeting each month. And yes, the two of them worked well together. *Energize* was the way Lucy had described their chemistry. When he presented the idea at the next meeting of the Worship Committee, everyone was quick to agree that it was a good one.

"IT'S SO INVIGORATING," Lucy said when she dropped off the order of worship for Sunday's bulletin, "the way our minds work together, our combined creativity weaving such a lovely tapestry."

Bill examined the typed copy. "Oops, you forgot the time of confession."

Her mouth formed a pout. "It's such a downer. Here I try through my prelude, the choir's invocation, and the opening hymn to create an uplifting atmosphere. Along comes the confession, which you've got to admit, Bill, makes us all—who wants to think about what we've done wrong and take responsibility for everything that goes on globally? Environmental conditions, racism, poverty. Why, in just a few minutes, confession undoes everything I've been working so hard to establish. See if anyone misses it."

It all made sense, the way Lucy put it.

IN THEIR LIVING room Wade and Elsie ate Sunday lunch off TV trays. Today they had much to discuss, Elsie being particularly effusive over Stan Acheron's visit to the library after church. Such a nice man, organizing a youth choir in addition to being youth advisor. He'd been sorting through his books, he'd told her. Could the church library use some of them?

And Stan Junior. Wasn't he a polite young man? That Evelyn was certainly a weird one, though, wasn't she?

As he did multiple times each week, Wade spoke of how much Lucy appreciated the work he did on their house. Such a kind young woman. And pretty.

The door buzzer. About the only ones ever to come around were Jehovah's Witnesses. Wade put an eye to the peephole. Lucy! He considered not answering the buzzer, but Elsie called out, "Who is it?" He turned back to her and put a finger to his lips.

"Wade! Wade!" Lucy called. "Wade, Elsie. Are you all right in there?"

What would she do if neither answered? Call the police?

Wade opened the door a crack. "Uh, hello Lucy. What brings you to our neighborhood?"

She stretched her neck to see inside. "Hi there, Elsie." She gave the door a gentle push and stepped inside. "I just came by to—" She turned her head side to side and gasped, "Good Lord!"

What no one knew: All these years Wade and Elsie would have welcomed visitors had they not been embarrassed. They'd never even spoken to each other about the matter.

At issue was the Victorian house they'd lived in for thirty-six years. Practically every item they'd ever owned took up space in its fourteen rooms. In the living room a single pathway led through piles of newspaper and magazines. Elsie served all their meals on TV trays because both the kitchen and dining room tables were stacked with dishes and knick-knacks. Frequenters of garage sales and flea markets, Wade and Elsie had, just that past summer, added eighteen pieces of glassware that Elsie found drastically reduced when the flea market was about to close for the day; a box of bathroom floor tiles exactly like the tile they had (in case any of their present ones ever broke); an eight-foot long table they could put their new purchases on; fifteen used picture frames; and four five-pound coffee cans filled with screws, nuts, and bolts.

Lucy stood there, turned her head to the left, to the right, down at the floor. Gasped. And laughed. A laugh unmistakable in its mockery.

THE FUNERAL WAS AN ESPECIALLY somber event. Neither casket was open, the bodies being charred and unrecognizable. The melancholy hymns Lucy played on the organ were all in minor keys. The choir sang Brahms's "How Lovely is Thy Dwelling Place."

Paradise Unraveled, Part II

In plain, then, what forbids He but to know,
Forbids us good, forbids us to be wise?
Such prohibitions bind not. But if death
Bind us with after-bands, what profits then
Our outward freedom?
Paradise Lost, Book IX, Lines 758-762

Aug. 8

I DON'T CALL THEM Father or Mother, for they do not act as parents are supposed to, that is with my well-being in mind, or even with a hint of affection. Neither do I claim a relationship with Stan Junior. God's Revenge, they say of me. I ignore them. To act as if they're irrelevant is the worst insult I can heap upon them.

I am a freak with the knowledge of a millennially old woman, the body and pimply face of adolescence. I'd say freak of Mother Nature, except my circumstances cannot be blamed on her. My fate is of my own undoing.

We have again moved, their ambitions in the last church accomplished. As always they left behind hearts broken, faith destroyed, seeds of distrust planted. Lies and lust prevailed.

Aug. 14

Daily they remind me that I don't belong. A loser in a family of winners. Lucy uses the word *disheveled* to describe me, comparing my hair to a wild vine, implying that I have no control over myself and that like a vine, my spirit must be pruned. Yet, were I like them I'd despise myself even more.

They appear forthright while they are in truth crafty; charming while in truth offensive.

This evening the three stood before me and accused me of disloyalty, to them the most loathsome of qualities. Even if your country practices bigotry and narrow-mindedness, even if it slaughters innocents in other countries, you're supposed to sing its anthem, recite words of praise, even die for it. This family demands the same. Sing its praises, never criticize. Die for it, if called to do so. Long live the king. Long live the dictator. Long live Stan and Lucy and Stan Junior.

It goes back to the pact agreed upon in the bowels of the earth, never to do good. An agreement I was not privy to.

Sept. 2

"The mind is its own place," Lucy reminds me. "You can make a hell of wherever you are. And you certainly seem intent on doing that."

I know their light-heartedness is feigned. They do not acknowledge the deep sadness they carry with them, the profound sense of loss. Lucy's laughter erupts too quickly, its edges like shards of glass. Stan has a ready wit and charm, which to the ordinary onlooker convey self-confidence and friendliness. But both of them live in a bottomless pit, where real beams of sun cannot penetrate. Only artificial light dwells there.

Sept. 28

They have brought their evil to a new target: Happy Corner Baptist Church. Happy until Stan and Lucy have had their way. The congregation is a remnant of its former self, with fewer than fifty members desperate for the spark of hope Stan and Lucy are all too eager to provide.

Every Sunday I watch Miss Slaughbaugh and her dog make a hasty exit. I've been curious about her disappearance at the end of every service, leaving before we've finished the last hymn. Why doesn't she want to talk with anyone? This morning

I followed her out. I planted myself between her and the long hallway. The dog, of course, came to an abrupt halt.

"Don't touch Freckles!" she commanded without knowing who I am. "You're not supposed to touch seeing-eye dogs."

Freckles tilted her head and looked at me in a sweet way.

"She's a beautiful dog," I said.

"Don't touch her."

"I won't. Has anybody ever told you what she looks like?"

"Caramel, they say. But what good is that if I don't know what caramel looks like?"

"Let me try."

She heaved a sigh. "If you must."

"What is the most beautiful thing you can think of?"

She didn't hesitate. "The London Philharmonic playing Beethoven."

"Freckles looks like a Beethoven sonata, harmonious and majestic. You know how sweet some strains are, and you almost want to cry?"

"Yes."

"Freckles looks that sweet and gentle. . ... You know how your heart feels when you hear a familiar overture, how it fills with love for the melody?"

"Yes."

"Freckles looks up at you, and she looks like that love."

"I see," she practically whispered.

"May I accompany you home, Miss Slaughbaugh?"

"If you must."

The taxi took us to a neighborhood near the city boundary, not far from the college I attend. We pulled up in front of a large Victorian house with a porch on three sides. Inside all was tidy and clean. When I asked if I might fix lunch, she said, no, her housekeeper had prepared something. She invited me to join her.

We didn't talk a lot, maybe because we're both used to having to keep our thoughts to ourselves. But when I left she encouraged me to return.

Oct. 7

It feels like Providence brought me to Miriam. (She wants me to call her Miriam, not Miss Slaughbaugh.) She has a conservatory, a magnificent room with a vaulted glass ceiling. In the center there's a small pond and a fountain spraying water over pebbles. She's filled the warm, humid area with a variety of plants. Bright pink bougainvillea climb a trellis. The sweet fragrance of Madagascar jasmine wafts in the air. As we moved from plant to plant she identified each by name.

"Why do you grow these if you can't see their beauty?" I asked.

"Even when nothing is in bloom, the air is filled with the scent of green, the essence of life. I touch the waxy leaf of the magnolia, the spikes of the quince. I feel dirt's potential to nourish the plants. And would you believe the plants speak to me?"

"Yes, I believe that."

It is as if I've returned to my true home.

Oct. 11

I visit Miriam regularly. Evenings we play dominoes in her parlor. She runs her fingers along the dots' indentations, then slides a piece in place. She said she doesn't remember when she laughed so much. I told her my life lacks humor as well.

We tend the plants too. Miriam says she's never *seen* anything like it, the way they respond to my touch and voice by sending out shoots and blossoms. One tree in particular, full-bodied with shiny leaves, has drawn our attention. She has run her fingers across its leaves, up and around the long rough trunk, and remains puzzled. Its height, extending all the way to the roof, indicates the tree is not young, yet Miriam says she didn't plant it. I'm quite curious too.

Oct. 14

Already members at Happy Corner think Stan is extraordinary. He teaches the youth Sunday school class. People comment on his being *down to earth* and a lot of fun. Lucy, with her musical talent, has organized a choir, a small group that sings her praises. My heart is breaking, for I know where this all will lead.

Over dinner tonight Lucy laughed about another success. "I told him it bothers me that he goes by Pastor Bill. 'You're a Solomon, you know that? I think you should insist on being addressed as Reverend Benedict, not this casual Pastor Bill.'"

I've seen her do it before, lure a man into believing he's God Almighty. This can only lead to disaster.

Oct. 28

I spent the whole day with Miriam, repotting plants, sinking my hands into the soil, getting dirt under my fingernails. I am reminded of a time when I felt at one with Earth.

This afternoon I happened to look in the conservatory pond. What I saw amazed me. She was lovely, the girl who gazed back at me. Her hair lay in soft waves around her face. Her complexion was smooth. Her eyes were bright and full of humor.

"Miriam," I asked, "what do I look like?"

She was on her knees, patting the soil at the base of an angel trumpet. She rose and walked to the chair she often sits in.

"What is the most beautiful thing you can think of?" she asked me.

"A breeze."

"Ah. You know how gently it strokes your face?"

"Yes."

"Your face has the same gentle quality. There is no harshness about you. You know how the breeze plays with your hat, blows a piece of paper out of your reach?"

"Yes."

"Your face has the same sweet playfulness. And the way a breeze lets you know it can be kind and gentle but it also has the potential to be mighty?"

"Yes."

"Your face shows your capacity for striking down something you know shouldn't be there. Think of the breeze as the breath of God. Your face, dear Evelyn, looks like the breath of God."

I rose and went to her chair. I lowered my body to the floor and placed my head in her lap.

Spending time in the conservatory with Miriam has brought back memories. Of a secret bower, the canopy of trees spread above me, a carpet of soft moss beneath my bare feet. My own special province, where I, not Stan or Lucy, was the favored one. In my memories I glimpse a time when I was happy.

I told Miriam about my special place. I did not tell her about Lucy discovering it, of her tempting me to eat the forbidden fruit.

Dec. 24

Except for a candle in each window, the sanctuary was dark, those in attendance full of anticipation. All was silent except for the swish of Lucy's long black taffeta dress, invisible against the backdrop of the darkness. Walking slowly, dramatically, up the center aisle, she carried a two-foot candle that illuminated the delicate features of her face.

When she reached the steps of the chancel, Harold Markham began to read from Isaiah: "The people who walked in darkness have seen a great light; those who dwelt in a land of deep darkness, on them has light shined."

Lucy, in her usual theatrical way, stepped to the altar, where she placed the candle in the wooden holder Wade Kirkakoff had made especially for her.

As she approached the choir, dimmed lights shown above the singers. There was a faint tone from her pitch pipe, the raising of her arms. From twelve diaphragms, mouths, and lips came melodic strains that most choir members would have, until recent months, thought themselves incapable of.

Finally—a grand finale it was—Lucy stepped over to the organ and as if magic were in her fingers and feet, pounded out the Halleluiah Chorus. After the service people swarmed around her, telling her they'd been moved beyond words, and what a great musician she is, and how lovely she looked tonight, and how the Christmas Eve service has never been so meaningful.

Evil can be so deceptive.

Jan. 20

I've been dreaming lately. Not nighttime dreams over which I have no control but daytime dreams, which I create to please myself. I'm moving out of Stan and Lucy's house and moving in with Miriam. I dream I sleep in the sunny corner bedroom upstairs that has organdy curtains and a dust ruffle on the bed. The bed frame is brass, the vanity and chest of drawers mahogany. Some of her furniture belonged to her grandparents.

How wonderful it would be to have ancestors. People who pass on to you not just furniture but a moral legacy as well. Everyone in the family would know that to be a Wilson or a Montgomery or a Bailey means you honor Creation, all of it. Theirs is a feeling of connection to a noble past.

I imagine having breakfast in the little nook off Miriam's kitchen, or studying at her dining room table. I hate the house I live in, with its imposing front gates of iron and the long, rutted lane through brambles. Even in winter, the vegetation surrounding the house is out of control, with thorny plants creeping all the way up to the porch railing. The house is as gloomy in daylight as in darkness. I want to escape.

Yet escape is impossible.

Jan. 30

A Beethoven sonata on the radio provided background music while Miriam and I played dominoes. I had built a fire in her fireplace. I liked the way it crackled and sizzled.

How did the topic of sin arise? I didn't intend to say much, but as one nugget of information slipped out, I felt compelled to add another, then another. I had a curious mind, I told her, which made me susceptible to seduction. Now I live with the consequences of my gullibility.

"You must free yourself of this guilt," she said. "There's nothing wrong with wanting knowledge."

I told how I paid a high price for my intellect. I am cursed. I am neither demon nor human. I will never have a full life.

A branch scratched against a nearby windowpane. In the fireplace a log dropped.

Feb. 17

It was inevitable. From the beginning I saw in Brad Hoffman a kind and sensitive boy. He stuck like glue to Stan Junior, and during youth meetings, whenever Stan Senior took the guitar out of its case, Brad rushed to be by his side. He was ecstatic when Stan offered to teach him how to play.

A week ago, Stan Junior made snorting sounds when Brad came near, and Stan Senior said in front of the whole group that Brad was a mediocre guitarist. Last night Brad put a gun to his head and killed himself. For years I've watched Stan and Lucy and Stan Junior at work. *How talented you are. How intelligent you are.* Once they are confident about the power they wield, they destroy the confidence they have fostered.

As I expected, Stan and Lucy have taken on the role of Comforters-in-Chief. They wrap their arms around Brad's mother, pull her to them, and encourage her to cry. They are sooo sorry. It is sooo tragic. But he is with God now, they say. It is God's will.

After the funeral, mourners will do as Stan and Lucy intend: They will hold God responsible.

Feb. 28

I'm positive Lucy had something to do with it. Two more deaths. Just about every week Wade Kirkakoff repaired something for her. He installed a new bathroom vanity and practically put in a whole new kitchen. He finished the basement so she could have her choir parties down there, and painted the living room—deep red, wouldn't you know. He worshipped the ground she walked on, practically drooled in her presence. I don't know what precipitated it, but a fire consumed his and Elsie's house.

Another funeral. Another chance for the Comforters-in-Chief to walk among members of Happy Corner and declare that the deceased are with God.

March 10

Lucy grabbed my sleeve, clenched her jaw, and spewed, "I just found out you've been going over to that Miriam Slaughbaugh's house. How long has this been going on?"

I was taken by surprise. "Since we moved here."

"What have you told her?" Lucy's beady, hate-filled eyes stared into mine.

"Nothing. We just talk about music and stuff." I know better than to mention the conservatory.

"It's a good thing she can't see what a pitiful creature you are. How weak you are."

She turned and stomped upstairs.

I'm worried. Lucy would like nothing more than to destroy what I love. I know what she is capable of. Vicious rumors. False accusations. Might she make up something terrible about me and tell Miriam, who is as attached to me as I am to her? Will Lucy get at me by breaking Miriam's heart? Freckles. Will she harm Freckles?

Miriam's survival depends on me.

I've always known I cannot escape. It would be futile to try. Though I've watched as they've worked their destructive arts, I've felt helpless to intervene. This time must be different.

March 15

Thorns scrape my arms and face as I drag the five-gallon container down the long lane. Later, in the middle of the night, I rise from my bed and quietly exit the back door. I take the container out of the shed, carry it into the house, pour gasoline on the draperies and sofa and chairs. I light a match and rush outside into the darkness. From a safe distance I watch the flames leap into the heavens. I feel the intensity of the heat.

I will never be free of them. But for once I recognize that I am not helpless. I will protect one I love.

Timbers crash. Sparks fly. Soot floats above me.

By the River Styx

For nothing lovelier can be found
In woman, than to study household good
And good works in her husband to promote.
Paradise Lost, Book IX, lines 232-234

IN ALL MY YEARS of marriage, the year I sold
Tupperware has been the happiest. Now isn't that something? A lady from one of the churches—I forget her
name—but she got me started. Probably knew how much I
needed the money. Selling Tupperware could fit well with being
the mother of four young children, and I'd be able to earn a
little money, at least get to keep the demonstration pieces.

Gordie was furious. He refused to mind the kids when I had
an event scheduled. He shouted that I was a terrible mother, a
selfish woman.

I hardly made a cent, only enough to pay the sitter and buy
my gas. But it wasn't for nothing. The best part was the
monthly meetings of sales reps at the Ramada Inn. In the
ballroom we ate chicken salad and croissants on white linen
tablecloths. The company representative, usually a man, gave
pep talks, and it occurred to me that for once someone was
telling me, "Yes, Lillian, you can do this. You're a capable
woman." The trainers told us to be creative in how we presented the product.

So I came up with this act. I decorated the different kinds
of containers like they were hats, and I'd get all the women at
the party to wear one, and I'd give them little scripts to read,
and everybody would be holding their sides with laughter.

One day Gordie came storming into the kitchen. He said people were talking about my silly parties, and he wasn't going to put up with my embarrassing him any longer.

I embarrassed him, humiliated him? As if over the years he'd done nothing to humiliate himself.

I really did love you, Gordie. I loathed the way you treated me, but I loved you anyway. What I wouldn't have given, just once, to hear you apologize for what you did to me.

GREENVILLE, LOUISVILLE, YORK, Baltimore. We moved in and out of towns as if they were railroad stations. A long orange van (sometimes a blue or white one) would pull up to the curb, open its double doors, and swallow the family's belongings, the history of four children embedded in the stains and scratches of secondhand furniture: a dining room table with *Property of the U.S. Air Force* stamped on the bottom, a chest of drawers I had taken from the curb in front of a neighbor's house before the trash truck could haul it away. Out of the parsonage and up the truck's ramp, muscular men carried boxes with Clorox and Napa Valley Wines stamped on the outside, their contents listed with red marker in my careful printing. One labeled *kitchen* contained CorningWare plates with service for eight and stainless-steel flatware I'd collected using grocery store coupons. Of course there were Gordie's books: commentaries and Bible dictionaries, works by Tillich, Bultmann, and Bonhoeffer, none of which he ever looked at. In years past, stacked atop everything, there had been children's tricycles. Then bicycles. This time only Matt's mountain bike made the move, though he was now away in college.

Gordie had again taken a new parish, necessitated, no doubt, by word getting out that he had something going with Pamela Atkins. The sprightly music director was always calling the parsonage, telling me, if I answered the phone, that she needed to *confer* with him—probably about whether she should play a hymn in the key of F or the key of C. Would the choir sound better with the sopranos on the left or right of the chancel?

The very name of his new assignment made me grimace: Happy Corner Baptist Church. I doubted that I'd be any happier there than I'd felt blessed at Blessed Redeemer.

SEATED IN THE chintz-upholstered chair purchased at a yard sale, I stared at the half-finished jigsaw puzzle. I had no idea how much time had passed since I'd last slipped a piece in place, only that the colors were now blurred, the tabs and indentations distorted.

"Now go upstairs and work on your puzzle," Gordie had instructed more than an hour earlier, as if I were a child, "and don't come down until I call you." He needed to hold his counseling session at home, he said. An AA meeting at the church preventing his using his office.

All was quiet downstairs. Not so inside my head, where scraping sounds sent chills down my spine. An occasional crash, like symbols striking against each other, made my body jerk. I needed my medicine. Now. But the bottle was on the kitchen counter and Gordie had told me not to go downstairs.

I had to stop the noises.

Deliberately I paused at the upstairs landing to bump the wall and knock a book off the table. In spite of the racket, my appearance in the living room seemed to surprise Valerie Peterson, whose bra, I couldn't help but notice, gave the appearance of her having three breasts, one at the base of her neck.

"I need my medication," I mumbled, looking straight ahead toward the kitchen, walking past the sofa where Gordie and Sally sat no more than a foot apart. Though I knew exactly where I'd placed the amber plastic container, I spent a few minutes aimlessly opening and closing drawers, running water in the sink, moving jars around in the refrigerator.

The puzzle upstairs. What was the picture of? Maybe an autumn scene with red and gold leaves floating down a stream. Or was it the Alps?

I left the kitchen carrying a pill and the glass of water. In front of Gordie and Valerie, I stopped to study her, starting at the wedged sandals of pink leather, up to the hem of the short pink skirt, on up to her white knit top clinging to perky breasts. The third breast was gone.

The Alps or autumn scene, or whatever, could wait. I took a seat in the rocking chair across from the sofa, put the pill in my mouth, took three gulps of water. "So how's Eric liking junior high?" I asked. The chair's movement consoled me: my head bobbing forward, my shoulders pushing the chair backward. Forward. Backward.

Turning to Gordie for a signal, Valerie cleared her throat as if preparing to speak. But it was Gordie who answered. "That's why she's here." He rested his hand on her knee. "We know all too well what that stage is like, don't we, Lillian? We thought Amy would never outgrow her sassiness. And Matt, our youngest. You wouldn't believe what he put us through." To me he said in a gentle tone. "Now go back upstairs, honey. Valerie's still got a lot to work through. Back upstairs, you hear?" I obeyed.

An hour later, bed covers tucked under my chin, I told myself, *Gordie's a minister, and counseling is part of his job. Sometimes it's with women. Well, most of the time. Women are that way, more willing to seek help. Heaven knows, getting a child through the junior high years* . . . I fell asleep.

"What the hell!" Gordie was shaking me.

I rolled onto my back, shading my eyes with my hand. "Huh?"

"You'd think that one place—at least I should have some privacy to work from home. It is after all church property. But no, my wife comes traipsing through the living room on the pretext . . . then sits down. Sits down right in the middle of a counseling session."

He reached over, grabbed the collar of my pajamas and pulled me to a sitting position. "Jesus Christ, why did you have to sit down? Then the rocking!"

"A woman's in my living room, practically sitting on my husband's lap."

The slap across my face knocked me back against the pillow. I raised my hand to check the sting.

"You slapped me." My voice was a hurtful whine. As cruel as he'd been all those years I'd often reminded myself, *At least he doesn't hit me.* Now he had.

"Well, you made me angry. Interfering with my job responsibilities, letting your petty jealousies take over your common sense."

"You slapped me." I rolled over and buried my face in the pillow.

Lying down beside me, Gordie gently stroked my hair. "Sweetheart, you know I don't want to hurt you. But you wouldn't lay off. You know I don't want to hurt you."

"Let's go see a marriage counselor. We've got to . . . we need to talk things over. Can we? Will you?"

I half expected him to respond with his public voice, the one I heard at church, a voice that conveyed sincerity and concern. But it was his private tone, with its snarl and nastiness.

"If you and I went to a marriage counselor, if we communicated honestly, the result would be—I'd leave you."

Everything was quiet, except for the clattering in my mind. I again buried my head in the pillow. *He loves me, he loves me not, he loves me, he loves me not.*

"Back to the issue at hand," he said. "You must never do that again, interrupt a counseling session. Do you hear me?"

Loves me, loves me not. The crashing of cymbals in my head.

"Do you hear me?"

"Uh-huh." *Please, God, make the sounds go away. Please. Please.*

Until I pretended to be asleep, he sat silently beside me, then tiptoed out of the room. Moments later I faintly heard his voice downstairs talking on the phone.

GORDIE'S BRIEFS AND T-SHIRTS lay folded in the laundry basket I clutched in my arms. *No one cares where I am,* I thought. *I could be down here in the basement for hours.*

What if I shrieked for help? Would anyone come? Would anyone care? The Boy Who Cried Wolf. I understand why he called out. He didn't think anyone loved him. He wanted assurance.

"Help!" I screamed as loud as I could. Again, "Help!" Overhead, footsteps thumped then came down the basement steps.

As soon as I saw Gordie's face I laughed uncontrollably. I let the laundry basket drop to the floor, watching, as if in slow motion, its contents unfold and land in a disheveled heap. While he stood over me, hands in pants pockets, I collapsed at his feet, hugging his calves. Still clinging to his legs, trying to make sure they wouldn't walk away, I burst into tears.

He grabbed my shoulders, shaking them so hard that my whole torso trembled.

"What the hell are you doing?"

Still I sobbed.

"Good grief." He pulled loose and walked toward the stairwell.

"I wanted to see if you love me."

Without a word he ascended the steps.

"I wanted to see if you love me," I whimpered after him. Still seated on the cement floor, I wrapped my arms around my knees and put my head down. The Boy Who Cried Wolf, what did he find out? Did he learn that the people you call will come, but their coming doesn't really mean much? Only that they can hear your voice if they want to. Most of the time they just don't want to.

"MARILYN BARBER," THE young nurse announced. The woman to my right stood and left the room. One after another our names were called, women wearing faded blue wraparounds held together by snaps, following technicians down the long hallway, where a machine would smash our breasts and take an image so we'd know who would live, who would die. No, the machine was supposed to tell us early so our lives could be spared.

Reaching over to the coffee table, I pulled out the most recent issue of *Redbook* and flipped through its pages from back to front. Magazines should put the table of contents at the end. That's the way I've come to see life: that we only understand later the pages that come toward the front. Only then can we decide what's worth looking at closely.

Eight women seated around an ornate coffee table displaying magazines we were supposed to find interesting: decorating hints, low-calorie foods, how to juggle parenting and career, PMS. Issues that no longer held my interest.

One article, though, caught my attention: "How to know if your husband's unfaithful." He's trying to lose weight; he's gone from boxer shorts to bikinis; a woman calls him on the phone and he takes the call in another room; he works irregular hours; he buys you a special gift. Where was this article ten, fifteen years ago? Would I have believed it? The proof I needed, all there, but I chose denial over truth. Had to believe him, for my own sake. Which proves my point about understanding life from back to front.

From years ago I remembered Alma Somebody, whose husband had been an alcoholic. She took his abuse for decades, all the while wishing he would die. When he finally did, she made plans. She would travel to Europe, move out of the house they'd lived in, buy a condo. She would join a women's book discussion group and make new friends. But Alma had attended only two meetings when she learned she had a rare disease. Less than a year later, before she journeyed outside the country, in the bed she had shared with her despicable husband, she died. *The same could happen to me. Even if I am among the lucky women here, I can't assume I still have plenty of time.*

Gordie had stolen twenty-seven years of my life, and time could not be retrieved. He'd squandered my love, and love spent could not be reclaimed. There were things I'd lost permanently, but myself I had not lost. Not completely. I'd be furious if I didn't live long enough to make up at least partially for what had been taken from me.

It was there, where women walked in and out of the room in blue cotton wraparounds, where some reflected on their past and others on their future, that I decided, firmly this time, that I could—*I would*—salvage what little sense of self-worth remained. I would not let Gordie destroy me.

I FOUND JIGSAW PUZZLES at garage sales, estate sales, sometimes drastically reduced at the grocery store. The picture on the front of the box didn't matter. When each piece finally interlocked with others, there would be a collection of multi-colored chili peppers, a landscape in Switzerland, a Van Gogh painting. A picture having so little to do with my life that I'd barely pause to study my accomplishment before pulling it apart and dumping it back in the box.

Each piece haphazardly falling, falling until it rested beside those from the other side of its world; sliding, jiggling, rattling, its jagged edges catching my flesh, ripping it until blood poured out, spraying the box's contents in crimson. Then the blood was seeping through the cardboard, dripping through the seams, soaking into the lid so that the picture of what the completed puzzle was supposed to look like was drenched. It had all disappeared: the photo on the box lid, the pleasant image of what was to have been my life.

Gordie said puzzles were a waste of time, that I was crazy. A conclusion I questioned less and less as the years went by, for I knew what went on in my mind in the silence of the evening. A swirl at first, of noises demanding one thing then another, of the phone ringing with some woman's voice asking, "Is Gordie there?" Then a leveling off, a low hum, not unlike that of a florescent light ringing in my ears. The hum would have me screaming except I knew it would go away, usually as I snapped a piece in place.

Then tranquility. My shoulders relaxed, my mind calmed, I would continue my effort.

THE KITCHEN WAS CLEAN and Gordie had left to do the Business of the Lord. Upstairs, seated in the chair, a gooseneck lamp illuminating the card table, I peered through the bottom of my bifocals. I turned each puzzle piece as if appraising a gem, working out of habit, noting protuberances and notches.

I fumed. Gordie bore responsibility for my pain. Controlling me, belittling me. Gordie, who pretended to be above reproach, all the while counting on my self-destruction.

Well, I wasn't an old woman. Chances were, I had several years ahead of me. I could be like the loaded gun in Emily Dickenson's poem: a deadly force that only needed an eye to the sight, a finger on the trigger.

Now my hands moved rapidly, joining pieces in rapid succession. Yes, I'd been waiting far too long, and now the time had come.

Of course, some would claim a divorce was the best solution, but a divorce would become a contest in which Gordie quickly seized the advantage. He'd end up with his job, his income, his reputation more or less intact, while I'd have nothing. No, I was going to win this contest. I was going to come out of it knowing I'd outsmarted him, knowing I was clever and powerful.

I would kill him.

How—that was the problem. No bomb in a letter. The day it was to be delivered would be the one day he would bring mail home from the office and open it at the kitchen table. Killing me too. I lacked the stomach for driving a knife into his heart while he slept. Face it, Lillian, I told myself, you don't have the stomach for brutality. Besides, you'd be substituting one life sentence for another.

Several white pieces with brown rod-shaped flecks formed a cluster.

Gordie had tried to kill me by destroying my spirit, every bit as ruthless as a gun placed at the head. Except no one else recognized it for the violence it was.

Six pieces of bright red with nearly microscopic brown spots.

There was a drop-off next to a nearby walking path that had once been a railroad track. Maybe I could convince him we should go for a walk, and when we came to that place, I'd take him by surprise and give him a firm shove. He'd tumble down in somersault fashion: head, shoulders, back, feet, head, shoulders, back, feet, until he lay far below. Lifeless. But what if I didn't—take him by surprise that is? He'd see what I was up to, and before I knew it I'd be the one plunging to my death. Besides, there was little chance he'd accompany me anywhere.

A cluster of peach-colored pieces went right here, and the light brown grainy section joined . . .

I could hire someone to tamper with the brakes. No sense bringing another person in on this. It would only increase the odds of getting caught. Carbon monoxide poisoning? The parsonage had an electric stove. Fumes could come inside the garage. Not likely unless I could hit Gordie over the head with a baseball bat after he was already in the car. But any coroner would recognize the crushed skull.

Too bad, with all those self-help books out there, there weren't any on how to murder a husband.

As I slipped the last piece into place, I dropped my hands to my side and leaned back in the chair. For once, I studied a finished project. One thousand pieces celebrating dessert: cheesecake, chocolate éclairs, torts decorated with glazed peaches and strawberries and tropical fruits. Mounds of whipped cream. The way to a man's heart is through his stomach. The way to a man's heart. Gordie's father's heart, Gordie's brother's heart. Gordie's already high cholesterol count, the thirty extra pounds he carried.

Who would suspect a woman of murder who prepared delicious meals for her husband? Gordie was already near the age his father and brother had been when they died. Maybe his arteries were on the verge of clamping shut, and all they needed was a high-fat diet. My patience could last awhile longer.

No doubt because frugality was a lifelong habit, my trip to the grocery the following day took two hours. I stood in front of the deli case shaking my head over the price of the best cheeses. Shivering, I hovered over the ice cream choices, searching for the brand with the highest fat content. It was nearly twice the cost of my usual brand. Could I afford to buy sour cream *and* creamed cheese?

Lillian, I said to myself, you have no qualms about killing your husband, but you can't bring yourself to buy the necessary tools. Revenge ain't cheap, woman.

THE SCENE IN THE BASEMENT, the time I called for help while doing the laundry, often comes back to me. Certainly, the location is a metaphor for my mental state at the time. I still cry for the Lillian who felt so isolated and lonely.

Nowadays I try to maintain positive thoughts. Not in denial but in celebration of what I've learned and the wisdom I can pass on to other women. Yet there are times when I get stuck in negativity. That's when I turn my mind to lessons a woman can learn from doing the laundry.

She learns not to overload the machine. It can only handle so much. If you cram all the kids' jeans in one load the machine will make a terrible racket when it gets to the spin cycle, or it might refuse to spin at all. You usually have to lift some of the jeans, by then waterlogged and heavy, and transfer them to a basket or a laundry tub. You spill water all over the floor, and then the machine may still resist returning to its cycle. You've ended up making a big mess, and you know that it would have taken less time and energy if you'd done two loads in the first place.

The same with a woman's life. People can keep loading her down, but at some point she's going to refuse to take any more. She may even break down altogether. When that happens there's a mess to clean up. The good news is that she's resisted. People may be furious at her for letting them down; they may laugh at her foolishness, but she's stood her ground. She will not allow herself to be overloaded.

Doing laundry also teaches a woman about static cling. Gordie's black socks were forever hiding in the back of the dryer. When my panties and blouses and skirts were put in, the sock always had to cling to something, spinning around and around and around, convinced it was having an intimate relationship, I guess.

At the end of the cycle, I'd pull the sock away and put it in the drawer, where it belonged. But then the next time I did laundry, that damn sock latched onto a blouse or a slip. It couldn't stand not to be clinging to something.

I used to believe evil has some mystical strength. Static cling taught me that evil is born of weakness. It was Gordie's weakness, not his strength, that created victims.

Paradise at Gun Point

"Revenge, though at first so sweet,
Bitter ere long back on itself recoils."
Paradise Lost, Book IX, lines 171-172

REVEREND GORDON FISCHER didn't see it coming. The congregation was standing in prayerful pose, eyes closed. Except for Valerie Peterson, whose flirtatious gaze met Gordie's. Oh, and Stella Hamilton, whose attention was focused on the postlude, a challenging work with three sharps. At Miriam Slaughbaugh's feet Freckles knew something was amiss and growled a warning.

". . . The Lord make his face to shine upon . . ."

Bang! Bang! Bang!

Reverend Gordon Fischer dropped to the floor in a heap. Before she realized it, Stella had played two measures, followed, once she saw what had happened, by a loud discord, a cacophony that only an organ of such magnitude could create. The forty-three worshippers were so stunned they could only remain standing, grasping the backs of pews.

No one saw the shooter. But by the time the police arrived, Freckles had led Miriam to the Cradle Roll room, where Helen Campbell lay curled up on the floor sobbing and hiccoughing. Two officers handcuffed Helen and led her away. Paramedics, after lifting the body onto a stretcher, covered it with a sheet.

Gordie Fischer was dead.

Police wanted eyewitness reports, but Miriam Slaughbaugh was blind, and everyone else's eyes, with the exception of Stella's and Valerie's, were closed, and Valerie wasn't about to provide any information about the glances passed between her and the minister during the final moments of his life. She was, however, distraught. Because he was dead and because she had a hunch she was somehow implicated.

Happy Corner members did not appreciate being detained, especially since, as far as an investigation was concerned, they had no information to contribute. Hank Melrose had promised to take his boys to the afternoon Orioles game. He didn't much like Reverend Fischer anyway. Connie Canknuckle was distraught over seeing the preacher's dead body, but preferred grieving at home, where she could cuddle with her dog, Cleopatra. No one thought to suggest that Lillian, the pastor's wife, accompany his body to the morgue, nor did she express a desire to do so. Neither did she want to hang around and pretend to mourn.

While stomachs growled, police officers insisted on speaking with each person present.

Q. Where were you seated?

A. I was in the fifth row. In the seventh. In the third row from the back.

Q. Did you hear the shots?

A. Yes. Yes, but I thought something was wrong with the sound system.

Q. Did you know the assailant?

A. No. Sort of. Not really. She was real shy.

HELEN CAMPBELL

For more than a year I'd turned to Oprah for advice. Over my lunch hour, by the wide faculty lounge window that allowed as much light into my spirit as it did into the room, I would sit in the olive-green vinyl chair, reading the self-help books she recommended. Highlighting passages, first with a pink marker, rehighlighting in yellow during a second reading, later with a green marker. By reading and rereading, I hoped to become a new woman and that the feelings of self-value Oprah spoke of would fall like a veil over me.

My goal was to become a spiritually evolved woman, one possessing the kind of love that inspired others to love me in return. I pictured myself with an expansive embrace, arms growing longer and longer until they surrounded every child I'd ever taught, every coworker, and scores of people I hadn't yet met. They'd be embracing me too, all these people. And I would be happy. Finally, I would be happy.

The other kindergarten teacher, Felicia, told me about the dynamic new minister who had come to her church over the summer. He was in his late-fifties, she said, not unattractive, though not handsome either. A casual style, that's what people liked about him. He wore khaki pants and Izod shirts and wasn't at all pompous. His sermons were down to earth, not theological mumbo-jumbo. They were short.

God, I'd long figured, was hiding from me. Hiding behind the cluster of lilac bushes out in the backyard where my mother beat me with a doubled-up belt and I called out for deliverance. Hiding behind the school clock I turned to as a child, seeking assurance that I'd soon escape taunting classmates and indifferent teachers. For most of my life, I figured God was hiding in Antarctica, somewhere very cold so I'd never go looking.

I'd been thinking that maybe it was time to move beyond Oprah. Why not check out the Happy Corner Church and this Reverend Fischer Felicia thought so highly of?

WIND SWEEPING ACROSS city streets nudged me to the steps. As I placed my foot on the first one, images of childhood gripped me by the throat. My psyche flailed. That woman would be inside, the one whose glittering gold jewelry could blind a person, like staring at the sun. The woman who carried a box of food from First Methodist Church wrapped in red and green paper with Santa Clauses all over it. "Merry Christmas," she'd chirp in a few minutes, tweaking my cheek, then tell my mother, "What a sweet little girl you have." A sweet little girl she wouldn't think of letting her own daughter play with.

In my hesitation to enter I took a moment to study the colossal doors of solid oak, a masterful work of art. Their intricately carved borders depicted scenes of Eden: Adam, Eve, the snake, and a tropical tree heavy-laden with fruit.

Oprah would understand if I turned around and left. I'd go back home, change into jeans, and resume reading *O*. Another Sunday. I'd ask Felicia to come with me.

As I turned to leave, an elderly, dignified-looking man in saggy pants and a misshapen sports coat held the door open. "Lovely fall day, isn't it?" he said, smiling. It seemed I was watching a movie in slow motion: entering the narthex, gliding down the center aisle—step, pause, step, pause. I saw myself as the young bride I'd once been, clinging to my grandfather. Step, pause, step, pause. Except instead of admiring me, people all around were whispering. "Look at her, look at poor little Helen." Clicking their tongues, they pointed out to each other that my clothes were shabby and I looked malnourished.

Desperate to escape their attention, I bolted into a pew near the back, bumping my purse against the woman who half stood to let me pass. Just as I was about to sit, I tripped. My hand landed on the crotch of the woman's husband. People turned to see the commotion.

What in heaven's name am I doing here? I have no business in the grown-up world. No business trying to blend in with respectable people. In a church of all places!

I tried to calm myself by closing my eyes and taking several deep breaths. When I opened them I saw mostly a blur of white: white walls, a white ceiling. Then I noticed details: wrought-iron light fixtures hanging from the lofty ceiling like dainty earring fobs, a massive organ with looming pipes, which I anticipated falling and wiping out everyone there.

Only then did I see that the crowded sanctuary was a product of my imagination. I counted forty-one adults and five children in attendance.

As the congregation sang hymns I'd never heard and recited from memory litanies I didn't know, I peered toward the front to get a better look at this Reverend Fischer. He sang without glancing at the hymnal resting on the paunch beneath his black robe. Instead, he gazed through black-rimmed glasses out over the sanctuary, periodically flashing an easy grin as if he'd made eye contact with a friend. There was an incongruity between the dignified bearing of his black robe and his relaxed, playful even, manner.

He preached on Samson and Delilah that Sunday, contradicting the usual belief that Delilah was a bad woman. She may have been a good woman, he suggested, who was attracted to a powerful man. Too often women were blamed for God's plans going amuck. Eve too. But God didn't blame women. God loved them.

His words were an inspiration to me. On my way home I imagined myself seated in my living room across from him and Oprah. Oprah would say how proud she was that I'd gone to church. I was taking courageous steps toward facing new realities. Reverend Fischer would again assure me that women—more specifically, me—were not to blame. God loved me. To which Oprah would add, "Love. That's what gives us the energy to evolve spiritually."

A PASTORAL VISIT, he called it when he telephoned to ask if he could stop by on a Thursday evening. By then I'd attended church every Sunday for six weeks, taking in each word he said about how God loves us all and how with God's help we can succeed at whatever we want to do.

I turned the word *pastoral* over in my mind, considering green fields like the ones in the painting over Grandma's sofa. Green fields with a gnarled oak tree off to the side, a couple picnicking beneath its branches. Most likely a pastoral visit would be pleasant.

But how to prepare? Would he want to read the Bible or pray over me? Maybe he'd ask a lot of questions: Had I ever been baptized? How long had it been since I'd been to a church? Maybe he'd quiz me on my religious beliefs. What if he asked what I thought about—what did ministers talk about? What if he asked what I thought about sin? I'd say it's . . . I'd say it's bad. Then I wouldn't be able to think of anything else, and he'd know I was stupid.

I had vague memories of a minister visiting my grandparents' house, but I never hung around long enough to know what the adults talked about. Later Grandpa would complain that the only time people from church came by was when they were asking for money. Good Lord, surely Reverend Fischer wasn't going to ask for money.

And what was a woman supposed to wear for a pastoral visit? I looked down at the light gray pants I'd had on all day, with spots of Elmer's Glue, a grape juice stain from Angie Halverson's spilled drink. Balancing on one leg then another, I stepped out of the pants into a black skirt that would go with the pastel blue sweater I already wore. In front of the bathroom mirror I applied pale peach lipstick and blotted it with a square of toilet paper. Briefly I picked at a pimple that had erupted on my chin since that morning. Oh, well, one advantage of having freckles was that pimples, at least little ones, didn't stand out. With a few flicks of the wrist, I pushed my bluntly cut straight hair behind my ears.

Grandma always gave the minister something to eat and drink. While a pot of coffee brewed, I arranged a dozen macaroons on a white plate. I took two Corning cups and saucers from the cupboard. I'd had fancy dishes once, a gift from Paul's aunt and uncle, but right before the divorce he sold them, along with most of our other wedding gifts. And kept the money. I didn't object. Nearly all of the presents came from his relatives.

Reverend Fischer was late. When he finally arrived, his appearance startled me, as I'd only seen him in his black robe. He wore gray corduroy pants and a steel blue sweater that matched his eyes. His ruddy complexion and heavy jowls reminded me of Dr. Lawson, a favorite college teacher. Reverend Fischer looked so—like a nice, very relaxed man. And I liked him.

He didn't ask about what I believed or didn't believe. "How long have you been teaching kindergarten?" he asked instead, taking two macaroons from the saucer.

"Eleven years, two of them right after college. . .. What I mean is I taught two years then . . ." Working around my life's mathematical complexities didn't come out right. "I've taught eleven years," I finally said, a little more emphatically than intended.

"Guess you've got stories to tell." Which seemed like an invitation to share one or two. I ended up telling three in all: about Laurie bringing a dead kitten to Show and Tell; another about Ross secretly passing his father's porn magazine among the boys; and one about David coming to school without having taken his Ritalin and before the day was over he'd knocked over the gerbil cage and poured animal cookies down the toilet.

Reverend Fischer laughed at each anecdote, his nose crinkling in a cute sort of way, while sounds like a gun's staccato shots came from his mouth. Behind the dark frames of his glasses his eyes narrowed into slits with branches of lines at the outside corner. For a moment I considered telling one of two more stories. Just to please him. The way I would later try time and again to make him happy—so I could see that expression on his face and know I was the reason.

"IT'S SO GOOD TO SEE YOU AGAIN." Just inside the oak doors, beyond the reach of December's frosty fingers, his steel blue eyes penetrated my hazel ones. His hands held on to mine so long that I still felt their warmth when I reached to open my car door. So good to see you again, so good to see you again.

And so good to see you too, Reverend Fischer, I thought as I drove my Honda Civic out of the parking lot.

Please, call me Gordie, he would have said as he leaned over to kiss me.

Now where did that idea come from?

"I think it's a sign," I said aloud, making a left turn onto Elm Street. A sign of my loneliness, the kiss. I knew it wasn't romance I wanted from him. He was a minister, married at that. It was probably God's love I needed to be sure of. The God who wasn't hiding in Antarctica but was peeking out from behind the altar of the Happy Corner Church.

FELICIA FARMER

You can't make up this kind of story: Pastor murdered on a Sunday morning right when he was saying the benediction.

I can't say that Helen and I were close friends. We both taught kindergarten at Dolly Madison Elementary School. She had a few years previous experience and was generous in helping me start my teaching career. I would never have imagined her murdering anyone.

Here's what police uncovered in their investigation: Helen and Gordie Fischer (no longer *Reverend* Fischer, in my book) were intimate. Police interviewed two other women with whom he was also sexually involved. Their names were not disclosed, though Valerie Peterson quit attending church immediately after the incident. Several of us assume that the third woman was someone he met while serving on the community's End Sexual Violence Task Force.

Helen believed her affection for him was reciprocated, this discovered through a letter she'd written but never sent. When she learned she wasn't his one true love after all, she bought a handgun and started practicing at a gun range every evening. Obviously, she was good. Three shots right to the heart.

Every weekend I visit her in prison. Strange how being locked up seems to placate her, mainly, I think, because the women respect her for murdering a man. The prison library has mostly true romance books, which depress Helen, her with no prospects for romance anytime soon, so I always take along ten books from the town library.

Gradually she's shared factors that precipitated the event. After three months of intimacy, during which Gordie declared his *undying* love, his ardor waned. One afternoon, he called to say he couldn't come to her house because he needed to be with a parishioner who was going through a crisis. Helen drove to the church, parked nearby, and waited until his little red Mazda Miata pulled out of the parking lot. She then followed him through city traffic to a Mexican restaurant. From behind a room divider screen, she saw him in a booth, holding hands with an attractive young woman. Not a parishioner, and clearly not going through a crisis.

Helen doesn't use the word *humiliation,* but I think that's what drove her to kill Gordie Fischer. She often says she was stupid to believe him.

The same self-evaluation can be said of the Happy Corner Congregation. Stu Campbell vows he'll never again serve on a search committee. You feel really stupid, he says, to assume you're getting the cream of the crop, only to discover the cream has curdled. He doesn't use the word *humiliation,* but it's humiliating to know that the denomination had so little regard for our small congregation that they sent a man so flawed.

Nobody speaks of Lillian.

Life at Paradise Acres

Happier, had it suffered him to have known
Good by itself, and evil not at all.
Paradise Lost, Book XI, lines 88-89

EIGHTY YEARS AGO ranchers owned much of Central Florida. I've been told that you'd drive through that God-forsaken area, flatter than a tabletop, and all you saw would be the sameness of wiregrass and saw palmetto, with Brahman cattle foraging for what nutrition they could find. Now and then you'd come upon a crossroads with a post office and a filling station. All of this pre-Disney.

Today the area's a mecca for snowbirds and us retirees. Tiny towns became cities, every one of them with a Walmart and McDonald's, a big mall where we get our daily constitutional during inclement weather—*inclement* meaning hot and humid. A short distance from the businesses, wide palm-lined streets have stucco-sided houses and clusters of condo buildings on both sides. Landscapers spread pine needle mulch on azaleas, camellias, and a variety of palms. Gators sun themselves along the shores of manmade ponds surrounded by green fairways.

Paradise Acres Retirement Community was established in such a town. It's for retired church workers, most of us former missionaries and ministers of a progressive ilk. Conservative retirees tend to choose Calvary Place or Holy Palms, farther north toward Orlando. At these places a person can get black-balled for questioning prescribed Christian beliefs, such as the Virgin Birth. Joanne Carlson, who used to live at Holy Palms, was shunned for commenting over Easter Sunday lunch that singing "Up from the Grave He Arose" always reminds her of a Jack-in-the-box. Then she laughed. That's reputed to have been the worst part, her cackle. After hardly anyone spoke to her for more than a month, she packed up her belongings and moved to Paradise Acres. Marie Packard came over from Calvary Place after she was reprimanded for quoting from the Revised Standard Version of the Bible. "If the King James Version was good enough for Jesus, it's good enough for me," she was told.

I'm not sure what it says that to my knowledge nearly all the people expelled from Holy Palms or Calvary Place have been women.

To be sure, we have our reprobates at Paradise Acres, but some of us venerate them as free thinkers. Mark Willoughby, for instance, who, after all his years as an inner-city pastor and hospital chaplain, reached the conclusion that God doesn't exist. Mark's t-shirts are as controversial as he is: *Thank God I'm an Atheist* and *Jesus Saves You—From Thinking,* among his collection. Mark spends each day presiding over a regular group of his challengers and supporters around a table in the Murphy Hall Lounge. I've attended a few times, but they argue like they're tackling a fresh topic when in truth they've repeated the same points a gazillion times. Their tempers get so on edge that Mrs. Harbold has to defuse the situation with chocolate chip cookies, which she keeps in a tin on a shelf behind the employee station. Maybe that's why the men rehash the arguments, so they'll get cookies.

Eleven retired female ministers meet once a month over tea. They're of that generation of women denied full membership in the Jesus Club. Supposedly, his hanging out with twelve men signifies a command from God that women can't be part of the Holy Circle. And did not the Apostle Paul himself exhort women to keep silent in church?

I quit the ministry after serving at what used to be called the Happy Corner Baptist Church. At Marsha's urging, I went back to graduate school and earned a degree in psychology. She and

I both taught at a Methodist college, which qualifies us for residency here.

The years have been kind to the two of us. We have few health issues other than my blood pressure and Marsha's getting a new hip last year. Recently she returned to the Get Fit as You Sit class. An itinerant beautician colors her hair the shade of strawberry blonde it was in her younger days.

We have an apartment on the second floor of the east wing of Albright Hall, with a balcony overlooking one of the three ponds. Weather permitting, I like to read out there, mostly mysteries, now and then a book I heard reviewed on NPR. Some days I can be found in the woodshop, where I turn burls into bowls. Marsha volunteers in the Paradise Acres library and knows practically every resident by name.

I guess it's part of getting old, the way a lot of us repeat stories about our younger years. Marsha and I have different explanations for this. I like to think it's because after all this time we recognize a compelling narrative, one offering a little mirth, a bit of wisdom. The past draws us like sugar attracts ants.

Marsha attributes the repetitions to the male ego. She says we men want to cling to the good old days, when our bodies responded to our wishes to compete in sports, when we had status and power. Whenever I start out with *Back when . . .* she asks, *What about now, Bill?*

OUR CLOSEST FRIENDS are John and Katie, a couple who found each other here. Katie graduated at the top of her seminary class, with aspirations to be a pastor, but had to be content with employment as a Director of Christian Education, because of what the Apostle Paul said against women speaking in church.

John's a retired minister from Ohio, a widower. I wouldn't know, but Marsha says he's good-looking for a man in his seventies, with intense brown eyes that can melt a woman's heart. Katie laughs at the suggestion that she and John get married; he's learned not to press her. It's not unusual, though, for him to answer her door in his robe. They've taken trips to Spain and Ireland. You get cheaper rates per person, he reminds us, if two people share a room. Then he winks.

Twice a week Marsha and I eat dinner with them in the fine-dining room. White linen table clothes and small vases with fresh flowers make residents feel like we're at a fancy restaurant. We have to provide our own wine.

The other night, I brought a photo album to our evening meal. "Look here, John. The cover's made of leather. Phyllis Baxter herself—a parishioner—she embossed our names on it."

Marsha's look was a scornful smirk. "He was miserable the whole six years we were at Happy Corner. You never heard a minister curse so much."

"Look, here's a picture of Marsha at one of the church picnics, standing next to her chocolate cake." I smiled at her playfully. "You were so cute."

She reached over and closed the album. "How about us reviewing the disputes? I swear, those people were forever arguing over one thing or another, especially when they were considering the move."

"It's called discernment, dear, not argument."

"Discernment my foot. There are no pictures of Hank Melrose's face turning beet red and his eyes bulging while he yelled that he'd worship in the old building till the day he died."

"Turned out to be the truth. The church didn't move until several years after we left."

"I saved your life, I did, convincing you to quit."

I opened the album again, pointed to a photo of the sanctuary's interior. "See what a beautiful building it was, but there was no way our little congregation could—"

"Kevin!" John knows all the waitstaff by name, their marital/partner status, what part of the globe their ancestors came from, and who their favorite singing group is. All four of us ordered the day's special: Flounder Florentine, roasted asparagus, and a green salad.

I hadn't finished showing off the album. I lifted it as the teacher of young children holds a book up so everyone can see the wolf, the castle, the ogre. "Look here, close-ups of these amazing solid oak doors. The carving was exquisite. *Is* exquisite, I should say, because they installed the doors on the new building. See. The luxuriant trees of Eden, the peaceful stream. Adam and Eve. The serpent."

Marsha wrested the album from me, placed it under my chair. "All right, honey, the church intended that someday, when we were old, we'd look at this and reminisce. We're old and you just did reminisce. Again, I remind you that you were miserable there."

I made sure my eyes conveyed a playfulness she couldn't resist. "See how heartless this woman is."

John poured honey-gold Sauvignon Blanc into each wineglass. "Here's to landing on our feet," he said, "both figuratively and literally."

"And to the medical profession for making it possible," Marsha said, pointing to her titanium hip.

The three—Katie, John, and Marsha—moved on to talking about the barbershop quartet's performance the evening before. Marsha and John disagreed over whether the tenor was off pitch, she complaining that her ears were in agony all through "Sweet Adeline," John arguing for forbearance, the high notes a challenge for an older man.

I knew what she was up to. She was trying to distract me, get my mind off thinking about Happy Corner.

I wish I'd not told her about the upsetting ruminations that keep me awake at night. "Just tell yourself to stop!" "Say to those troubling thoughts, go away!" Easy for her. She'd not been taken in like I was.

So while Marsha, Katie, and John moved on to other subjects, laughing and talking, talking and laughing, the persistent tape of regret played over and over in my mind. *Work it through, work it through, work it through.* As if I could go back and undo the past.

I foolishly hadn't anticipated the photo album triggering my strong feelings of shame.

"Do you believe Satan is real?" My question brought their lightheartedness to a halt.

"Do I believe evil exists?" Katie asked.

"I mean, do you believe in evil incarnate?"

Marsha, sensing where I was headed, said, "Please don't go there, sweetheart."

I repeated the question: "Do you believe in evil incarnate?" Not waiting for an answer, I continued, "I've never told you the precipitating event for my leaving Happy Corner, what made me finally say, I'm out of here."

"Which I'd been urging him to do long . . ." Marsha's voice faded.

"As I've explained before, it was a dying congregation. One Sunday this couple and their two kids—the boy in high school, the girl in college—they show up for Sunday worship."

Marsha placed her hand on top of mine, affectionately rubbed the corrugated metacarpals with her thumb.

"I was suckered into thinking they were the answer to prayer. Bring in some new blood, and the church would grow. They were a really talented couple. Lucy taught organ at the college out in the suburbs, and Stan taught ethics. He volunteered to be advisor to our youth group of four kids. Who volunteers to work with youth? Before long the group size had tripled. Lucy volunteered to organize a choir, leaving me to wonder where in hell would she find singers? In the whole church there were only forty-five members, plus six children."

"*Took over* the music program being the operative words." Marsha removed her hand from mine and reached for her wine glass, more to twirl it in sympathetic nervousness than to drink.

"Meanwhile, Stan, who played the guitar, organized a youth choir. The teens invited friends to be part of it. Even three Black kids from the neighborhood came. Everyone in the church was thrilled."

Just then Kevin delivered a basket of warm dinner rolls. I took one, not to eat but as an alternative to wringing my hands. My attention focused on the roll, I put a butter patty on it. Spread it. Spread it some more, before I looked up and gazed in turn from one of my dinner companions to the others.

"What I want to tell you, it's about my own—evil can be so seductive. I didn't have the wherewithal to recognize it. Or maybe—no, I was too trusting, gullible. So one day Lucy comes into my office. She was all the time coming to my office. On the pretense that we needed to plan the next Sunday's service, or—"

"Tell them what she was wearing." As much as Marsha had tried to discourage me from introducing the subject of Stan and Lucy, she now was invested.

"Yes, yes. She came in wearing a short red dress that, ahem, revealed a lot of leg."

"And you know Bill. He's always been—"

"For God's sake, woman, give me a chance to tell this the way I want to."

When I erupt like this, Marsha goes for the stare-down, clenches her jaw, and looks me in the eyes. Fortunately, Kevin approached with our flounder about then.

As he walked away, my voice took on a fake feminine tone. "'Isn't it fantastic,' Lucy said, 'how many people have turned out for the choir? And don't the voices blend well? You know, in just this short time I've come to love it here at Happy Corner. Oh, and Bill, your sermons'—here's where she clutched at my vanity—'I must say your sermons are filled with so much wisdom. Every Sunday I can hardly wait to hear what you're going to say.' She was all the time telling me what a gifted communicator I was and how I was like Solomon, and before you know it I'm thinking yeah, I'm amazing and nobody else values my eloquence or leadership, not even Marsha."

Marsha said, "Tell them about the chair."

"I'll get to that. Will you let me tell the story? Please!"

"Well, in case you've forgotten, I've been part of this marriage for over fifty years. So it's my story too." She got teary, which reminded me what a cad I am, even though we've talked all this through so many times and I've said scores of mea culpas.

"Is everything okay, folks?" It was Kevin again. "Is something wrong with the flounder?"

"No, no," the four of us chorused.

I apologized. "We're just so—you could say we're preoccupied." While he refilled our water glasses, we all took bites as assurance that everything was all right.

"This part is especially embarrassing," I continued. "One day Lucy told me, 'It bothers me that you aren't held in higher esteem. Like the informality of calling you Pastor Bill. You should have a title befitting a man of your education and experience. You should wear a robe instead of a suit and insist on being addressed as Reverend Benedict, not this casual Pastor Bill.' And I'm thinking, yeah, I deserve to be treated with more respect."

"I couldn't help but be disgusted," Marsha said. "It was like Bill had a personality implant. I was furious over what an arrogant SOB he'd become."

Katie asked, "So how long did it take you to see through this . . . this Lucy?"

"Actually, Marsha was the one to—after I told her about Stan coming by one day. His visit turned out to be the precipitating factor for my leaving. When I told her about it, she saw through their modus operandi. Stan and Lucy's. It was Lucy's job to build up my ego, his to tear it down. So this one afternoon he didn't bother to knock, just walked in my office and took a seat. Leaned back and spread out his arms and legs like he owned the place. He started telling me how he was counseling Roland Martin. Wham! I felt hurt, indignation, annoyance. Why was Roland turning to Stan for counseling when I was the pastor?

"He starts to tell me—so much for maintaining confidentiality. He tells me that Roland and Holly are having marital problems. He obviously delighted in his unorthodox counseling method. He'd told Roland that he needed to exert his manhood, that women are sexually aroused by—"

Again, Kevin approached. Again, he saw that we'd hardly taken any bites.

"I'm sorry," I told him, pushing my plate away, "I've lost my appetite."

"As have I," Marsha said.

John and Katie looked at each other. I knew they were hungry. "You two, go ahead," I told them. But they both signaled that Kevin could take their plates too.

"So what exactly did Stan tell Roland?" Katie asked.

"That women are aroused by take-charge men. He advised Roland to throw Holly on the bed and tear her clothes off her."

"Why that son-of-a-, that son-of-a-gun!" John scratched his head. "I don't get it. Why'd he tell you? Didn't he know it was a sleazy thing to recommend?"

"Worse than sleazy," Katie said. "Unethical by any professional standards."

Marsha looked at me through the top of her bifocals. "Now may I talk?"

I reached toward her. "I'm sorry I've been harsh. Sure. Like you said, you've been part of our marriage for fifty years, and you're the one who finally saw through them. What do you want to add?"

"Things started to happen. Roland and Holly got divorced. One of the boys in the youth group took his own life, and there was a girl, a high school girl—I noticed she'd put on some weight. Apparently, Stan was the one who got a call from the hospital saying she'd had a C-section. Not that her getting pregnant wouldn't have happened anyway. What bothered me was that Bill got locked out of people's lives. Everyone was turning to Stan and Lucy."

Katie took her dinner napkin from her lap, crinkled it on the table. "So, whatever happened to them?"

"Fire," Marsha said.

"Fire?"

"Yes, their house burned to the ground. No bodies were ever found, but the whole family—all four of them, poof. Disappeared. Strangest thing."

Marsha reached for the wine bottle, divided the little that remained among the four glasses. "Let's end the evening on a happier note, shall we?" She's that way, hesitant to dwell on the unpleasant. Besides, she probably didn't want me to play this nightmare video over and over in my mind at bedtime. So I was fine with changing the subject.

"A few years after we left—how many, Bill? Three or four? Anyway, Bill was invited to officiate at the funeral of Stella Hamilton."

I reached under my chair for the photo album, located Stella's picture. "A saint if ever I met one. The church had this huge pipe organ. Back in the day when they were prosperous, they could afford to pay an organist, but by the time I got there, the budget was tight and there was no money to pay anyone except me. Stella volunteered even though it was stressful, her not being an accomplished musician.

"You know, more than forty years have gone by since I left, but that woman stands out in my memory. If there was a need she'd find a way to take care of it. Someone to fill in for a Sunday school teacher at the last minute? Call Stella. One summer the camp was in desperate need of another counselor. Stella had never gone to a church camp and had little experience working with kids, but she went out there for a whole week. When I asked her afterwards how it went, she said, 'Oh, I can't complain.' Shortly before she died, the pastor died suddenly—"

"He was murdered," Marsha added, "and they hadn't yet hired a new one."

"Murdered!" Katie and John said in unison.

"That's a story for another time," I said. "Anyway, since we lived only about fifty miles away, they asked me to do the internment. There was a big turnout—about a hundred and fifty people, hardly anyone I knew. But that's how much she meant to so many people."

I felt my throat tighten. My eyes got misty. "It just occurred to me—not all my memories of Happy Corner are negative. There were some good people there. And you, Marsha, you were by my side."

I reached over and kissed her cheek.

The Tree of Wisdom

THE YEAR I TURNED SIXTY-FIVE my husband left me for a thirty-four-year-old blond; my boss at Wilkshire, Durham and Cooke asked when I planned to retire; and bus passengers started offering me their seats. Worse than any of these, however, was my sense that I had become an uninteresting person.

It hadn't always been that way. At social functions during my younger years I could count on being involved in a whole evening of interesting conversation. It wasn't unusual for me to be in the center of the most riotous group, people laughing so hard that everyone who wasn't in the cluster eyed those of us who were with envy.

Once the Happy Corner congregation moved out to the suburbs, closer to my home, I started to attend, as did women and men who were college professors, doctors, lawyers, a judge even. Church social gatherings became frequent. Was it that the other new members held more prestigious jobs or that I was now in my sixties and thus irrelevant?

I became aware of people handing me over. That is, I'd be sipping a glass of fruit punch at a celebration—a wedding, a milestone birthday party, Pastor Alice's induction as minister of Happy Corner—engaged in what I considered an interesting conversation about that week's programming on Public Television, when the person I was chatting with would stop someone walking past, introduce me, and walk away.

Rather like a slight-of-hand trick, where the card is there, then it's not, and you don't know how it disappeared. I'd be talking to one person and without warning suddenly find myself with somebody else. With equal frequency I would be exchanging pleasantries, when the other person would grab someone who happened to be walking past and begin a conversation as if I weren't even there.

All of this was quite disconcerting, as I'd long considered myself a good communicator. And an interesting woman. One who could discuss the Topics of the Day. One who knew how to keep a conversation going. But I seemed to have lost the knack.

I began searching for ways to make myself more interesting. At Oda MacFarland's one-hundredth birthday party I spent the whole evening in careful observation, wandering in and out of small clusters or standing off to the side and eavesdropping. Several times I noticed men talking about themselves. They explained how eager students were to sign up for their classes, how the business deal they'd just made was a stroke of brilliance, how they'd sailed the Pacific solo, or with what prominent person they'd attended the opening of the Orioles' season. Meanwhile, around them, two or three people signaled their admiration with wide eyes and pats on the back.

Maybe I'd been wrong all those years, asking questions and introducing interesting topics. Perhaps the secret to having people gather around you was to talk about yourself.

So, at the Strawbridge-Anderson wedding, as I balanced a cube of cake on a paper plate with a cup of pink punch, I exhibited a new behavior.

I approached a cluster of two or three people. "I had the most remarkable experience," I would say, then describe my hike in the Grand Tetons back in 1995 or my lunch with the president of the local chapter of the League of Women Voters. At first my new method seemed to work. People hung around. So I kept talking. About my new shower head, about how the kids who attended the school down the block littered when they walked past my house, about the new coat of paint the man next door put on his shutters, and about my most recent medical checkup. After a while, eyes glazed over and I was left with but one listener, who as slyly as a card shark, traded me off to somebody walking past. Who in a matter of seconds handed me off to someone else.

How was it that Dean Moser, founder of the newly formed Lite Steps Diet Plan, and Marshall Hancock, Chief of Police, could gather people around them by talking about themselves, but I couldn't?

Individuals telling a good joke were always surrounded by listeners. I went to the local library and checked out numerous joke books, searching for ones of the highest quality. I copied twenty onto index cards and memorized them. When I worked out at the gym, I carried three or four note cards with me, repeating the jokes over and over as I climbed the Stair Master and used the rowing machine. I told jokes into a tape recorder, which I played while falling asleep, for I'd read of how the subconscious mind hears and remembers.

That spring was characterized by several social events to which I was invited. "Did you hear the one about . . ?" I would ask Dr. Farnsworth or Ellen Singletary or Hampton Goodman. I found that listeners would laugh at two or three jokes then fade away. Or pass me off.

PASTOR ALICE'S OFFICE was a comforting space, with a deep cushy sofa and two brown leather chairs. Books filled floor-to-ceiling shelves along two walls. Along a third wall hung framed prints of drawings by Jewish children imprisoned in the Terezín Concentration Camp. Photos of Pastor Alice and her partner, Clarisse, adorned the desk.

I leaned forward in one of the leather chairs so that my feet, which I crossed at the ankles, reached the floor. Pastor Alice sat back in the matching chair. She's a tall woman whose feet reach the floor.

"Am I old?" I asked bluntly. I wanted her to say *no*.

A surprising question, it appeared to be, and one she considered carefully before diplomatically answering, "When does one become old?"

I shrugged my shoulders. "They say you're as old as you feel. I always thought that implied that you do all you can to take care of your health and stay chipper."

"Hmm, chipper. Do you feel chipper?"

I told Pastor Alice that I'd spent nearly a year searching for a way to remain chipper, but I constantly found myself on the social fringes, which made me feel like a non-chipper presence that dragged people down instead of up. I'd even tried telling jokes—to no avail. All the while Pastor Alice nodded her head in understanding.

"Now this is just me thinking out loud," she responded. "I don't mean to disparage your chipper thesis, but it seems to me that teenage girls are chipper. I look at you and I see an intelligent woman. And a woman who's accumulated a lot of wisdom. Telling jokes—it's like you're hiding your light of wisdom under a bushel."

My light of wisdom?

She stood and began to pace. Her Birkenstocks pressed a path near the edge of the area rug. She muttered several *Mmm*'s. Finally, "Seems to me the church ought to be able to provide a venue where people can share their wisdom, their life experiences. Speaking for myself, I've a lot to learn about how a woman navigates through a man's world. Like you did at the firm where you worked. I'd wager there are others with different areas of knowledge and experience." She stopped in front of where I sat, reached down, and placed her hand on my arm. "How does that sound?"

I didn't need convincing. I clasped my pastor's hand. "If you float the idea around, I'd be glad to help organize something."

That is how Pastor Alice and I became associates in developing the monthly intergenerational dinner.

An event Thelma Mabry would regularly attend.

Paradise Affirmed

*P*ARTNER, THAT'S WHAT Pastor Alice calls the lady who lives with her. As if they're cowgirls or work together on *Law and Order* or are with the same business firm. Clarisse is the *partner's* name.

"What a waste," Dallas Hines has said about Clarisse. Only to the old timers, certainly not in the hearing of members who've joined since Happy Corner moved from downtown to the suburbs. She's real pretty, Clarisse is. Blonde, with a stately posture. If he were forty years younger, Dallas says, he'd bed her and change her mind about liking women. That's what he claims.

Thelma tries to imagine what two women do in bed, as there's no Tab A to insert into Slot A. It occurs to her that she never gave any consideration to whatever kind of knicky-knacky Pastor Bill and Marsha, or Reverend Gordie Fischer and his strange wife, Lillian, engaged in. Homosexuals are different. Whatever they do, it's not natural.

She tries to remember intimacy with Alton, he with a Tab A for her Slot A. Thirty years he's been gone. So long ago that even with his picture on the bedroom bureau she doesn't recognize him. Can't remember what he was like in bed either. She loved him, that she recalls. So much that after all these years his betrayal still feels like a knife stuck in her ribs.

Thelma's attended Happy Corner Baptist Church ever since Mama, in her white gloves and plumed hats, dropped her off in Cradle Roll. Each Sunday Daddy, in his charcoal gray, pin-striped suit, held council at the foot of the church steps, offering his opinion on matters of local and national importance. Thelma and Alton were married at Happy Corner, the most prestigious church in town back then, with its genuine

95

Tiffany windows, elegant pendant chandeliers, and chestnut beams supporting the cathedral ceiling. After Alton's stint in the Navy they returned, he to take on the role of head usher, she to sing in the choir and teach Sunday school.

But for more than twenty years Happy Corner avoided the inevitable. Three and a half million dollars, the contractor estimated. A new roof. Major work on shoring up the foundation. Forced to realistically add everything up, the faithful found themselves subtracting instead. Subtracting members. Four of the seven final departures had tithed.

Thelma cried over the decision to move out of the city. As did Stella Hamilton, who cried, "What about the organ?" The beautiful stone building dating back to 1881 was sold to a struggling theater troupe for a pitifully low price.

The new church, located in the suburbs near Wentworth College, is an architectural nightmare, a pseudo-contemporary structure of pastel green concrete block. A cross perched atop a steeple-like platform lights up at night. Thelma misses the beauty and majesty that used to fill her with awe and reverence.

Yet forty new members joined within the first year. Professors and administrators at the college. More than twenty students. Nothing short of a miracle, some claim.

No miracle but a liberal takeover, Thelma thinks. The college people object to singing hymns with the word *blood* in them. No more of "There is a Fountain Filled with Blood." The liberals don't like songs about washing away sins either.

Well, after eighty-two years Thelma knows a thing or two about sin. Alton's affair was a sin. There's her longtime friend, Louise, whose husband beat her. A sin. Her friend Harvey Gladstone lost an election because his opponent made up a bunch of lies. A sin. Yes, Thelma could tell these liberals a thing or two if they bothered to ask. Sin is real.

And now a lesbian pastor. Not that Thelma was fond of Pastor Bill. Boring Bill, he was. So what *did* he and Marsha do in bed? Nor was she taken in by Gordie Fischer.

A lesbian pastor!

Dr. Hessinger, head of the college biology department, chaired the search committee. He testified to Pastor Alice's skills as a preacher, counselor, and administrator. Had anyone bothered to ask Thelma, she would have told them that the denomination doesn't allow gay and lesbian clergy. Turns out the liberals don't take to being Baptists anyway, and before you could say Howdy Doody the congregation was out of the denomination. So now, even though they're not on a corner, they're just the Happy Corner Church, and Thelma, for the first time ever, finds herself no longer a Baptist. Can't sing hymns about blood. Can't talk about sin. May as well be a Unitarian.

Word of hiring a lesbian minister has spread in the community. Local TV channels gathered outside the church on Pastor Alice's first Sunday. When Thelma watched the evening news on TV, she saw that the only people interviewed were those who think Pastor Alice is the cat's meow. Nobody asked Thelma. She would have told them that she knows a thing or two about sin, and homosexuality is a sin and she prays every day that Pastor Alice will repent and sin no more. That's what Jesus would say.

Letters to the Editor in the local newspaper have denounced the church for going against God's laws. A lot of "Adam and Eve, not Adam and Steve" remarks. The whole business is an embarrassment.

Willard Hapwell, who teaches art at the college, designed a logo: "We All Belong," in the middle of a pink triangle. He said it means that race, ethnicity, and sexual orientation do not disqualify anyone from being an active part of the fellowship. The logo has been made into pins, stickers, and a banner that hangs to the right of the chancel. Somebody handed Thelma a pin. She doesn't wear it.

IN THEIR BI-WEEKLY physical therapy sessions Allen doesn't treat her like the old lady she is but like a special person. He makes her think she can accomplish any goal they set together. Lift those weights, stretch that hip. His smile lightens her heart. Yet he stood before her one Sunday, greeting her in that sweet way he has, and introduced Vince, the man standing beside him. As his partner!

Pastor Alice and Margie Abbott have organized a monthly intergenerational dinner and made a point of welcoming older members, even arranged transportation. This evening Vince is in charge of the program. Elbows on the podium, he leans forward in intimate conversation. "During high school, in the locker room I figured that no one would know I was gay if I told crude jokes about fags. I was the brunt of my own jokes, and I hated that part of me. The gay Vince."

He speaks of his gratitude for the acceptance shown him at the Happy Corner Church. Thelma's eyes water as she thinks back to her years of teaching and remembers boys taunting each other. Was there a Vince among them?

"O FATHER AND MOTHER of us all," Pastor Alice prays. Thelma doesn't close her eyes as she was taught to. A habit carried over from the old church, where she looked up at the stained-glass windows and absorbed the peaceful scenes: the meandering sapphire blue stream, sheep grazing in the pasture with its variegated hues of green.

Here the windows are squares of clear glass. An ancient oak tree stands outside the window near her. A scar, oblong and blackened, reveals where a major limb broke off. A heavy branch stretches parallel to the ground, extending outward like a bench. The tree's brothers and sisters are gone now, some chopped down for firewood or to make way for suburbs, others struck by lightning or eaten by termites. How did it happen that this tree alone survived? Thelma figures the tree, now standing alone, has had to adapt after having been part of a forest of siblings.

"Amen."

In front of Thelma a woman not much younger than she is places her arm around another older woman, gives her shoulder a squeeze. There is something between these two, a bond. Have they had to love each other in secret? For years, decades?

Thelma opens the supplementary hymnal containing what are supposed to be songs for modern times, with none of the old familiar ones. Good lord, a guitar and drums accompany this one, and in a tempo so fast she can't keep up.

The song ends. There's the rustle of bulletins, the bumping of supplementary hymnals returning to racks.

Suddenly the sanctuary is eerily silent. Thelma looks to the front and blinks in bewilderment.

At the foot of the steps leading up to the pulpit, an unknown man faces Pastor Alice. Boldly, solemnly. He has on a navy-blue suit, white shirt, and striped tie. In his right hand he clutches a Bible to his heart. In his left arm he carries a little girl, no more than three years old, who wears a pink organdy dress with puffy sleeves and black patent-leather shoes. There's something menacing about the man, the way he scowls, his thick black beard, his piercing eyes.

The two women in the pew in front of Thelma move closer together. In front of them Allen protectively puts his arm around Vince. The new organist looks as if she's watching a horror movie, her eyes wide open, her jaw gaping.

Pastor Alice rises from her red-cushioned seat. Later she'll admit she has no plan. Should she shake the man's hand and welcome him to the Happy Corner Church? Or kick him in the groin? She steps across the dais toward the intruder—for that's clearly what he is.

He raises the Bible above his head. "You are an abomination unto the Lord."

He turns to face the congregation, his voice intimidating. "How can you call yourselves God's people?" he thunders. "You have turned from righteousness. Leviticus 18:22: 'Thou shalt not lie with mankind, as with womankind: it is abomination.' Also in Leviticus: 'If a man lie with mankind as he lieth with a woman, both of them have committed an abomination;

they shall surely be put to death; their blood shall be upon them.'"

By now the ushers, two men and two women, have come up the side aisles to the front of the sanctuary. Pastor Alice shakes her head a gentle no.

"Let him say his piece," she says.

"'For this cause God gave them up unto vile affections,' the apostle Paul tells us, 'for even their women did change the natural use into that which is against nature.'"

Thelma's dumbfounded. Does this man think he speaks for God, thundering up there with his Moses voice, his confidence that he has the right to decide who's going to hell?

He places the little girl on the floor and again raises the Bible high, this time with both hands. "'And likewise also the men, leaving the natural use of the woman, burned in their lust one toward another.'"

The child, her eyes downcast, steps away from him a few paces. Out of nowhere Marie Rivers reaches out and draws her close, allowing her hand to rest on the girl's shoulder.

"Read your Bible, people. To ignore God's word is to choose the everlasting pit, the fires of hell." Here the man shouts: "THE WAGES OF SIN IS DEATH!"

Thelma, who considers herself an expert on sin, looks at the two women in front of her, at Allen and Vince. At Pastor Alice, on whose face there is no hint of anger or fear. That woman, Thelma realizes, that woman has been called by God. Thelma gazes up at the banner: "We All Belong."

Without considering her actions she stands, thrusts her shoulders back, plants her feet firmly. She reaches for the hand of one of the women in front of her, who stands and reaches to her right for her partner's hand. Who stands and reaches in front of her for the hand of Allen. Who stands and reaches for Vince's hand. Who stands . . .

Thelma begins to sing. "Blest be the tie that binds/Our hearts in Christian love." Others pick up the strain. Hands joined, all of the worshippers move to form a large circle. They surround the man and little girl.

Thelma's eyes fill with tears. She looks around to see others take tissues from pockets, wipe their cheeks. We all belong. That includes her. She belongs to this group of people who stand here, hands joined, singing and crying. And they belong to her. Her whole body feels indignation melting, the chards that have scraped at her core for years floating into the ether, giving way to a softening. There is no place in her heart for anger or condemnation.

Not even condemnation of the man who now stands in the middle of the circle. He takes hold of the child's hand again. His tone softens. "God told Jonah, 'Arise, go to Nineveh, that great city, and cry against it; for their wickedness is come up before me.' But Jonah did not . . ."

He seems suddenly to realize that he's surrounded. He looks from side to side, confused.

"Our fears, our hopes, our aims, are one," the congregation sings in robust voice, "Our comforts and our cares."

The man breaks through the circle, pulling the little girl behind him.

Everyone turns to watch him leave. On the back of his jacket someone managed to place a sticker, "We All Belong," within a pink triangle.